Black River

Anomaly

An anomaly deviates from a norm, is difficult to recognize or classify. *Anomaly* is a series which publishes heterodox, eccentric and heretical works. Mashing fact with fiction, poetry with philosophy, fish with fowl, *Anomaly* is a laboratory of unprecedented writings.

a re.press series

Black River

Justin Clemens
Helen Johnson

re.press Melbourne 2007

re.press

14 Henry St, Seddon, 3011, Melbourne, Australia
http://www.re-press.org

© Justin Clemens & Helen Johnson 2007
The moral rights of the authors have been asserted
Database right re.press (maker)

First published by re.press 2007

National Library of Australia Cataloguing-in-Publication Data
A catalogue record for this book is available from the National Library of Australia

Black River.

ISBN 978-0-9803052-2-7

I. Justin Clemens II. Helen Johnson
(Series : Anomaly).

Designed and Typeset by *A&R*
Typeset in Warnock and Arno

Printed on-demand in Australia, the United Kingdom and the United States.
This book is produced sustainably using plantation timber, and printed in the
destination market on demand reducing wastage and excess transport

To Paul Ashton & A. J. Bartlett

I am commencing an undertaking hitherto without precedent and which will never find an imitator. I desire to set before my fellows the likeness of a man in all the truth of nature, and that man is myself. Myself alone! I know the feelings of my heart, and I know men. I am not made like any of those I have seen.
— Jean-Jacques Rousseau

If it were possible that a person should give a faithful history of his being from the earliest epochs of his recollection, a picture would be presented such as the world has never contemplated before.... But thought can with difficulty visit the intricate and winding chambers which it inhabits.
— Percy Bysshe Shelley

Whoever looks at the insect world, at flies, aphides, gnats and innumerable parasites, and even at the infant mammals, must have remarked the extreme content they take in suction, which constitutes the main business of their life.
— Ralph Waldo Emerson

The first thing I remember is that I had climbed from my cot over the bars and under the constellations of animals that howled above like the stars in their celestial spheres. But as I was too young to know lions and snakes and monkeys and goats, I knew them only as anythings, frightful smears that whirred and clacked and spun. I knew too the spongy mat of my bed, the rasping wood of the bars, the vertigo of the animals. Out I climbed. I ran around and around the room, beyond the bars and the endless swing and rock of the false animals suspended from the ceiling that was high as any sky might be.

I remember the sounds, the feet and voices outside, outside the room of my cot and my freedom, and I knew that I should be behind the bars for the good of us all. I ran to the cot and climbed like I was climbing a sheer abyss that plunged downward forever. But my feet were slippery on the rungs. I scrabbled and scrabbled for purchase with my scrabbling feet, as behind me the sound of the heavy feet and the voices grew and I panicked as I felt the air of the opened door behind me and the breath of those people heavy heavy on my little neck as I fell screaming to the cot that had not held me. For they had seen me and they too were screaming that I had not been held and were enraged. And

I remember sitting on my father's knee looking out the window at the waterfall outside and the green leaves falling too like the water and leaf and water falling as he spoke. He spoke a poem that I remember still but do not know whether he spoke it wrong or whether my memory failed, whether it was his speaking or my memory or perhaps both. It was only later in the factory that I rediscovered the poem and found they were not his words. Or rather I discovered a poem that was so like it and so old that even my father could not have spoken it first. It was a poem by a lord and the poem as I remember went like this, she walks in beauty like the night of cloudless climbs and starless skies and all that's best of dark and bright meet in her aspects and her eyes thus mellowed to the tuneless light that heaven to gaudy day denies. But

that is not what the lord had written though that is how I remembered my father say it. Someone had got it wrong or deliberately changed it but there is now no telling who or why that was. That is my second memory, though neither it nor the first are at the beginning, not even the first. My third memory is of playing with myself beneath the sheets when I should have been sleeping. I did not want to sleep but there was nothing else to do. I did not sleep. What I felt for the first time was not panic nor the warmth of something in my father's voice as he misremembered or cha-

-nged the words of a little poem but a darkness inside that I would feel and have felt again and again like the cosmic darkness of a drive that is wrong and yet without which nothing. Who could say why that dark drive that has nothing of nature about it still pulses inside so attenuated and yet so forceful. Along it will run like a river forever. The pulse or beat of that drive could only be one thing, but it is found in all things, senseless and inexhaustible and unbearable. The many things in which I later found that same excitement you will hear as I come to them. They are the true substance of my tale, for there that pulsing thing is in them

though it may not look like it is there. But it is. It is. It is there. It is there more than you or I are there. It is there in all that's best of her aspects and her eyes and the cloudless climes though it is not the best. It is something else, as they say, something else. That is what I tell you, anyway, like the judges, the lawyers, the reporters, the court, even the strange woman with the teeth who made a little dry sucking sound as she typed as if she was indeed typing and not just sucking sucking at her own palate like it was not dry and like she would have the taste of herself to herself and no one else could have it. It was like she had been sucked dry, whether by herself or another I cannot tell. I wonder if she had been sucked down and now there was nothing left for her but the sucking itself, as if she were still there to be sucked

in her mouth by herself. Is that why she sucked sucked sucked at herself like that? But no one can know from looking at another what has been sucked dry and what still runs in them, for people can only look other than they are. They cannot help this. This is just how things are. There is no point in cursing or crying or calling down retribution upon their heads for not being what they look like. Though you scour all the signs for signs of what they are, you could not decipher them. You cannot help this. It is not your fault. Some people lament this state of affairs and some people take it for granted and others want to bring it all down like pillars of stone or pyramids of ice about their blind eyes. But pretty much all in all you cannot tell how people are going to go when the penny finally drops and all stands unmasked as if lies had been told. That is not very fair. Even when you try to tell them the truth despite everything, even if you could not say it though you were saying it nonetheless and they could not have heard even if you had done. Even when the pennies drop

from their eyes or from their ears or wherever pennies drop from. It is certainly not from heaven. No matter what people think, they cannot help thinking awry. It is delusion on delusion in there, I think. That is why you must attend to who I am so you do not mistake the lie of myself for the truth of my tale. The sucking woman is just one person about whom I worry, although that is unnecessary perhaps. I worry too about the man who was the student of my father and seemed to like him very much. But he hated me. For some reason one day he grabbed me by the scruff of the neck and shook me till I barked and whimpered like a little doggy that wants only to wet itself a thin yellow drizzle from its pizzle trickling on the soft white fur of its underbelly. Then he said so that everyone could hear, look, look at the little doggy with the funny tongue which wants to lick my feet, wants only to lick my feet as if it had been born to it. Everyone cheered and clapped and hoo-

-ted as he pushed me down to the ground still whimpering like a little doggy and stood there proud as you like while I kissed his feet. Though they were the first feet I kissed, or at least the first that I remember kissing, they were not the last. For everybody knows that other people are often other people who want their feet kissed, and to have others who will see them as the sort of people who have and like having their feet kissed. For some people this is all they ever want. There are other people, too, who like to kiss feet. They must somehow feel that they are so big or so small that they are untouched by such kissing, or by others seeing them kiss other feet. Some even say that this is a sign of sacrifice, of a self-sacrifice that saves. For self-abnegation or, shall I say, this ablative love that loves to prostrate or supinate itself as if on a stage, well, that is one thing that many,

many love to do. I must say, though I have kissed many feet, I have never really enjoyed it. I would much rather not have kissed those feet if it had been possible. I lament that it was not not possible. Admittedly some feet have no longer been attached to their erstwhile possessors, being as one might say detachable feet, but that is by the way. After all, feet are as feet do, organs of the body, and there is no reason why you should get on with your organs. There is no reason for your organs to like you, you the parasite of their labours. The organs of others may be best. I should also say that many

have kissed or at least tried to kiss my feet, and, might I add, certain other orifices as well. I cannot say that most times I have enjoyed that either. On the contrary, there is something bad when that little tongue comes out and the eyes look up and there is even the hint of a smile as that little tongue comes out at a trot like a bloated slug and runs its slimy trails across your arch and between your toes. The feet are what you walk upon if indeed you walk, but few do these days. For why walk when you can sit and sit and sit instead. Or for that matter lie. Perhaps for those who sit or lie having one's feet kissed is pleasant. I do not find it so. I would rather neither kiss nor have my feet kissed. As I have said

sometimes also they want to kiss more than your feet. I have lost track of all the places that people wished to put their tongues in my body, where they wished to lodge something of themselves. It is undoubtedly kin to that that black excitement or excrement I spoke of before. Which, when I think of it, turns up again and again in everything like a river of nothing running through a hole. Anyway, I have told you of my first and my second and my third memories, and also of the memory of kissing feet, though that is not the fourth memory though I told it in fourth place. The fourth memory is another sort of memory altogether. It is of a situation that recurs always with different figures, for example with the shaved man or the judge or the woman who sucked at herself or those who lapped at my feet. It is a memory that comes after the others as it comes before. It is a memory of what happened to people before my birth, and even before theirs. Kissing perhaps is not the worst of all, although

it is bad. People want it so much they would do anything

to keep kissing kissing kissing. Though no one wants to say that this is what they want, this is what they want. I have stood and said this until I have turned blue, for kiss kiss kiss is what they want. It is also what they do. This is no less true of my parents than it is of the court where I am standing or sitting. There is much kissing

in this trial. You may not admit it, because, as I have said, people always give other signs than they really are. People do not look like other people inside. They all have different powers and lights and if you like myself are sometimes capable of seeing what they are, though even I am very often blind to the truth too, you would not recognise the world at all. Some people are very small but they have teeth and claws. Others are all mouth without excretory organs. They can only eat and eat, and when they do they puff up and are in great pain but cannot stop themselves eating. Thereupon they only puff up more. Yet others have powers indescribable for those who have eyes, but are something like tentacles and beaks and tasting apertures that gleam and clash and, slowly, but with consummate delicacy, reduce their victims to ribbons. Those others, their victims, will scream and cry and flail about in the most exquisite agony although they do not realise

who or what it is that is causing them such pain. Yet there are creatures still more horrible. Some can take you and keep you alive, though you have become part of them and do nothing but their will, and they suck you till you are withered like an old hag. Perhaps it all begins with the kiss. But perhaps not too, as some do not have mouths, or have sewn themselves up so as to become desiccated sewers for whatever was inside. In any case, we are all like this and do not know it. I wish I knew what I was. But I cannot see myself in a mirror for, as vampires are said to do, neither do I find myself reflected there. It is the same here in this court that is filled with all manner of horrors. I hear one of them shouting while his little white curls like a little lamb curl about his little ears, what drives a man to kill another for as we know all men are brothers and brothers are a family business.

I can only smile at him, for he is like the lamb with his little curls, as are his brothers and sisters, even the one who is my friend. At least she says she is my friend though her voice is a bleating and the curls curl around her head too like those of a bleating lamb. They are connoisseurs of the kiss, but also of the blade. They ask for evidence. There is evidence. Creatures come and go. They bleat and squeal, they kiss and flense. Even if you see them you cannot see them all. I saw one kiss another on the feet just as if he were a kisser of the most acceptable kind. He kissed and kissed, and I nearly nodded off with the boredom and the distaste. But then I nearly screamed for that kissing tongue was not at all the slab of soft pink flesh I expected but a metallic claw with little hooks and grapples and he ran it up the leg of the man with the feet who was squealing and squealing though none saw nor heard nothing and he castrated the man and swallowed the black little testes just like that plop plop then disembowelled him right there and then, and then the glistening tongue was withdrawn into the mouth and out came something else like a fat

straw and he guzzled and guzzled at the other's innards though the other screamed and screamed and scrabbled uselessly with his useless hands as his belly was guzzled up through the other's straw and disappeared god knows where. All the while the sucking lady kept sucking as she did, and the white curled cadres bleated and bleated as they did, and others kept on doing what they did while the man was disembowelled before me. None saw nothing, not even the man with the metal contraption for a tongue, who did not even know that that was who he was or what he did, though that is what he was and what he did, for I saw it with mine own eyes. This is my fifth memory. It is not like one two or three or like four, which is, as I have said, different in kind from the others. This fifth memory is the memory of what is happening to me now if the present can be said to be a memory and I think indeed it can be said to be so. The present is a memory which i-

-s a memory of incarceration. I think if I would jump from this cot in which I find myself I would be free again in the enormous room of my first memory. But I do not think I can, because this is a palace of memory, the most ferocious and exacting of all the memories that there are, and that is the memory of the present. It is ironic, I suppose, that the present present is about memory, about where I was at what time and what I was doing there and then. For the bleating curls and the sucking woman and the man with a claw for a tongue want to know what I have done. I tell them about the feet that need to be kissed, and the

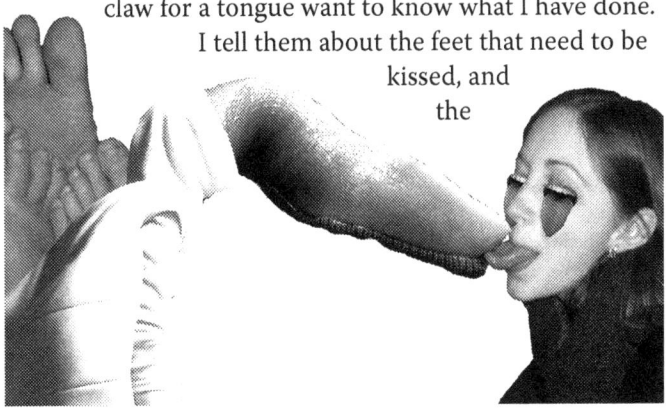

persons who need to kiss, but they will not hear of it. Feet, they say, are never kissed, except perhaps in private between two consenting adults or perhaps by naughty children who are incapable of knowing what they are doing. But children are not incapable, I would say if they could hear it, no, children are like dark aureoled shadows in which the future is growing like a constellation of lips and tongues. Children are not the people in this court, for they have not yet become, and this not-yet is a reservoir of power though it is dumb and unfocused. Children can kiss and kiss and not be sad or wounded,

though even their kissing still has that dark river running through it, that river of darkness that will not be crossed though you have all the silver in the world. I know there is no boatman. I have not seen him, and I have seen now almost everything. The persons in the court now ask me again about the feet. I tell them again about the kissing, but there is no comprehension amongst them. Which reminds me of my sixth memory, or rather my fourth kind of memory. Not one two three or four, the memory of others' repetitions, or five, the memory of the present, but six, the memory of what has not happened. Six, the memory of what has not happened, is because people are signs of themselves that are wrong. This is the memory, the only memory, that matters to people. What has not happened is true for them. They do not believe that they are kissers, though they are. What they believe are fairy tales, of this, then this, then this. They demand my memories of what has not happened. I must tell them, as I tell you, and they go something like this.

In telling the memory of what has not happened, the act of memory itself orders the events. The order of events is, like the events themselves, not of the world. Things do not happen one after the other, as if a billiard ball had hit the next. Things happen all at once and remain other than they are. There are no records of what happens, only of what did not happen. Or what fails to keep happening. Well, what did not happen to me began at the age of seven. I think at seven, anyway. It began with a theft. Or perhaps with a rape. I was in the garden, staring through the rough pile of rocks that was the fence separating the gardens of the houses of the village from the schoolyard. There was that day in the garden a woman gardening. Two other women emerged from a rough shelter in the garden, and grabbed the first woman. They spoke to her about something that I could not hear. She remonstrated with them. They tied her by her hands to the tree. One held her legs apart, and shoved her habit up above her belly, which was gyrating and contorting in fear just like the disembowelled man in the courtroom I described before.

The remaining woman began to shove the pole of the rake into the tied woman's hole. She screamed and screamed. The screaming was so loud I was certain that someone must soon come, but nobody did. I felt suddenly and unaccountably that dark river that I had felt in bed in the afternoon as a child. I took out my penis and shook it as I watched the women through the cracks in the rocky fence. I cannot remember how it ended, though I thereafter saw the tied woman again. She was one of the first people who I saw for real and not just as the wrong sign of herself. She was not as she was before, though I do not really know how she was before. She was now a glistening vessel shot through with red veins that pulsed without issue and force, though they remained somehow bright like a thing you would find in the nest of a crow.

I told everyone the story of what I had seen. They did not believe me, and I was beaten. Only one of my friends believed me. So we took another friend and tied him to a tree and thrust a stick into him again and again like the two on the one. Then I felt the darkness. I looked at my friend. He was like the golden sun about which my father had told me, pulsing like Apollo at midday. He looked at me and was the sun. He knew as I looked at him that I was like the eagle that can stare unblinking into the sun, and I knew then that he was a murderer of souls. Yet I was not scared. He needed one like me that he might be great, that I might admire the sun in him that others could never see. I knew that I had eyes then that were not the eyes of others. Perhaps they were not really eyes at all, but senses without names or organs, pure senses, senses of the real. I saw like an eagle flying sees through the sun and sees even the merest creeping thing that creeps upon the earth before it descends.

My friend had not these eyes. He had something else, the aureole in which children are suffused, and though the river of darkness flowed through him too, it would not hold him. I wonder how it is possible to speak of my eyes and his glory and the strange swelling of a feeling that remained inside but nonetheless coiled between us like a torsion of bonds that have been violently severed yet still are bonds, and which shine with a black burst of light that is something greater than the bond itself. I speak of this severing-binding through a third party, which is what we shared, I the witness, he the poker, and our victim, all three of us holy and sanctified by the unjustified suffering so great that the feeling could only be shared. Shared it was by my eyes, the light, the murderer of souls, and the screams and pleading that rupture the air, the light. Great

occasions rupture the light and the vision that is for all.
But greatest of all was the child who suffered and who now
lives forever only in the remains of bonds, curling and
crackling, their ends frayed and ashen by the unbinding
we had effected together. You must know that those who
act, act as the puppets of those who cannot speak or show,
they must bear the glory, as well as the shame for the bond,
the bond in its rupture at the heart of us all, a broken knot
slipped around the unrestrainable. And this time we were

worse than beaten. I would never see him again. When
imprisoned, I had my first visitation from the other side of
the black river, for humans never go there though the river
runs through them, there are creatures from the other side.
They do not stay on the other side, however. They are not
limited like us, they do not have to travel only this side or
along the river. We can drown in that river, they cannot.
They come and they come and some which you see are
those creatures of the other side. They are not even like the
man with the claw for a tongue or the thing with the beak
and tentacles or the sucking lady. The other things are like
my friend like the sun for they will eat your soul

and not just your body. Even the most voracious on this
side of the river eat only bodies and beings. These do not
murder at all, only preserve. Their preserve is the preserve
of the soul. This, then, is my seventh memory. After one
two three all one which are my memories alone and four
the memory of the repetitions and five the memory of the
present and six the memory of what has not happened and
seven the memory of messengers from the other side. The
messengers are sometimes described by others who are
captivated by six the memory of what has not happened,
and they are right in this because the other side does not

happen, but they are also wrong because they believe that they are of the type memory six rather than seven, which is something altogether different and there are not words. The creatures of the other side are like human beings in that each one is its own species, as different from each other as a fish and an image of a fish, or a sucking lady and the words sucking lady, but which is more real is not to be

said. This is the same again as between creatures of the other side and human beings. They are different genres as tragedy and comedy or romance and action are different genres. But you cannot describe or show in tragedy what a comedy is, or in a romance what action is, because the action in romance is not the action of action, but all the little moves of the face and little actions and reactions of the two bodies which circle each other like knife fighters who will never fight but whose encounter is in the circling without meeting, whereas action is the unavoidability of bodies meeting and bodies meeting is always a murderous clash that eviscerates. The kissing that I spoke of just a short while before is not comedy or tragedy or romance or action but something that all these turn about and refuse to tell the absoluteness of. Still, in some way, all want to speak of the creatures from the other side. I tell you that they visited me for the first time when no one knew what was to become of me becau-

-se I was so young. No one believed me when I said we were only repeating what I had seen in the broken heap of rocks that divided the gardens. No one believed me when I said that my friend had shone like a sun which only I could see. No one believed that the third whom we had poked with a stick was a sacrificial beast for us and beloved of the world, and was not unclean, and was not hurt by us though everyone thought that that was what had happened though it had not. Not everyone is such a thing that they might be sacrificed as the world demands. He was, in any case, poked, not kissed, which is something altogether different. All around I saw them kissing but few were willing to do any poking. Though I have since seen many such as the man with a claw for a tongue, and many, many far worse than he, at that time I was still young. I had seen only kissing and poking, aside from what I have spoken of my other memories.

Yet to go back is to go forward into uncertainty and invention. Even remembering what I did maybe a week or so ago is very hard and probably I was not attending very well to what I was doing as I was doing it. I was thinking about other things and would never have thought again upon it unless I had not thought that I had not thought upon it and now perhaps I cannot care less or just do not know if I care or not, or, perhaps, I am racking my brains to remember and the very racking ruins the memory and I realise that even as I rack and ruin I am not there, there where I try to think, and recalling it I am doubly not there and because it is hard to admit that makes it three times that I am and am not there. There is nowhere, is nothing, and my straining and racking is what there is. That is the point of which I spe-

-ak when I say I am not true. But truth there is, we all know it, and the truth abides. No matter what. What happens does not destroy but builds what is gone like a cathedral or a charnel house or a channel of loss for this slippery nothingness that flows through the hole of you. The truth that is gone is still.

So I must tell you of the first visitation from the other side, when I fell not into sleep, but into a state that was not quite midway between sleep and waking, but something like that. All of a sudden the room was lit with lights that whispered and buzzed like the experience of anxiety, when all your nerves tremble and your heart burns like a moth in flame. Yet these were nerves outside my body though they felt like they were within. They spoke all manner of things they themselves did not understand, for they are like devices that record and repeat without comprehension. Every soul they murder lives inside and babbles on in the lights, just as if it had been recorded, though the recording is rather an engulfing. Each creature of the other side smells of the rot of souls that now are nothing but their memories.

These souls have no further way of getting memories so they rot as they repeat forever, without any escape into death. Such creatures swarmed and buzzed about me in the room in my state that was not quite between sleeping and waking, but was neither. I heard all manner of things that no one should know but everyone does, even if they deny that they know. The murdered souls inside those creatures babbled of kissing as if it were the most haughty and elevated of things, because, as I said, they could now only repeat, and what they repeated were their memories of kissing before their murder, that did not kill but preserved them as rot. They lamented

their bodies, though they did not know they were lamenting because they rotted as they repeated, and it was strange to hear old ways of kissing repeated. It seems strange not only that so many kiss and kiss, but that they do it in such strange ways. It is because of these creatures visiting me and hearing their stolen souls repeating that I know so much about things that I should not. People have always been afraid of how much I know about them and their affairs, but it is only because the murdered souls of their families and friends have rotted before me in the whistling lights of the creatures of the other side. I am sure that the creatures visit others other than I on this side, but I have never met such another. I cannot be certain why I have not met at least one other who has heard murdered souls babbling in their room. Neither do I understand why they have not tried to

murder me like they murdered others. I think that somehow they need a witness to their voracious gobbling of souls. I am that witness, perhaps, to the gobbling of souls of the creatures of the other side who come. I think maybe they have somehow protected me from the kissing of others, for kissing makes souls vulnerable to being gobbled. You can look into the eyes of those who have spent their lives kissing and being kissed, and know that they are vulnerable, though every sign speak against it. This is why I cannot repeat too often that every sign that every human betrays is a wrong sign, and sometimes you may even come across a case of someone whose sign signs that it is wrong. That signing sign is a talisman against kissing, though the bearer will not know it, for the last thing one can see is oneself. This is true too of me, though I see so much, for, as I said, the self does not reflect. There is no mirror for the self, for

the self has no image in the present. Anyway, I remember that first visitation. There have been so many since then that I cannot remember them all, although some I would rather forget but cannot. While still in the cell that first time, I had another visitor. He was a living being which all the others kissed and kissed. I had never seen such a being before, and I have never seen another like him. For though they kissed him, he accepted their kisses as simply something that needed to be done for him to do what he had to do, but the kissing itself was not for him. He was, he said, an ambassador. I did not know what that meant. He accepted kisses, but looked otherwise. His head was a monster's, and from his body which was patched and quilted together from all sorts of creatures like dogs and cats and salamanders, blind fish, extinct birds, ancient and scaly reptiles, as well as still other beings, grew probes and long tendrils, which sprouted and waved in a rhythm whose principles were difficult to discern. Into my body he inserted probes. One tendril was directed up my nose, where I could feel it moving in a measured and intentional fashion. He opened up my navel with another, and felt about inside in a similar way, a quizzical expression on his features. After

some time, he finally smiled and withdrew his probes.

Then a mouth on a stalk emerged from his trouser leg and moved through the air like a snake until it was nestling by my ear, where it spoke in a voice so thin and tenebrous that, despite its closeness, I could barely hear it. The mouth whispered into my ear that it knew me, and that we would have a long and productive relationship with each other, although no one else would understand just what it was we would have. We are like a hole and a peg, it said, you the hole that our peg will plug, and together we will be a seamless unit though it seem we are enemies forever. Then the mouth withdrew, leaving the trace of its burning spittle to trickle through the whorls of my ear, where it would never stop burning to remind me always of the promise that had been made. The ambassador was very pleased. Everyone kissed him when he said that I was to be saved, and they kissed him again for his graciousness. When he had gone, they made me kiss them in all places.

Although he had made a point of telling them that they were not to do that, I could tell that he did not really care whether they did or did not. What they did was nothing to him. They were mere kissers, and he was not, and I was not, and that we both knew. They did not know, which is why they made me kiss them again. They threatened me with things I knew that they could not do, because I had now heard the strange and secret mouth on its stalk, and still felt its spit burning in my ear. They would not touch me, for they were terrified of the ambassador, and, although I was nothing to them, he had taken an interest, as they themselves said, he had taken an interest. Finally, they moved me from my cell to another. I knew no one in this new place, and nor did I recognise the sorts of beings they were. Many were kissers who pretended not to be, and others were not, though they pretended to be. Some

looked like nothing special. Some looked like my lost
golden friend, and were forever trying to poke others with
sticks. One of them tried to poke me, but when he did his
glow ran away from him along the stick and into my body,
which quivered in ecstasy. He screamed and screamed.
When they finally came to find him, they found him
twisted and charred, burned like a leaf in a forest

fire. He was never very good afterwards. His glow never
returned, and he had not even the heart left to kiss, let
alone poke. All the pokers thereafter regarded me with
fear, and the kissers tried to kiss me. I tried to ignore
them though their tongues were lapping at my body every
waking, and maybe for all I know, sleeping moment. As for
the others, they were such as had strange eyes and organs
dotting their bodies, for which there was no apparent
purpose. They had extra teeth and hair protruding from
their orifices, as if they were growing, or perhaps had
engulfed, other bodies. They were not at all scared of me
for the most part, but would sidle over and try to rub their
parts against me. Often this gave me pleasure, at other
times pain, but in no case were they able to engulf or
assimilate me, though I do not believe that this was what
they wanted either. In all of them I could sense the black
river running deep and wide

and fast. They were closer to it than any of the others. It
did not frighten them, but gave them powers that others
would try to lap away with their tongues, their tongues
that writhed like slugs that have fallen into a bath of salt.
Their powers were not as could be seen, but all sensed
something in these beings with their extra teeth and hair.
To tell the truth, these were more alien to me than all the
others, even the creatures of the other side, who at least

came to show me their engulfed souls rotting. When I had remained in that new place for a while, I was told I could return home, to my parents and loved ones, and so I did. But when I got there, they were no longer there. No one could tell me where they had gone. One said that they had moved away a long time before, and another said that they had all been killed in a fight, and another said that they had been ordered by the ambassador to go to war for the country, and another said that they had just disappeared slowly from sadness, until only their voices remained and then even those had slipped away. When I saw that I could believe

no one, and that there was no place for me there, among signs that were so clearly wrong, I turned the house upside down. For it was still there, as if occupied even though it had been abandoned. I found my old clothes which were too small, and my father's clothes which were too big, and my mother's clothes which were the right size but not right. So I tore up and tied together these clothes until they could fit me, though they were ungainly and strange. I found too some jewellery that I put on, and took some money, and went off down the road to find my fortune as people say. At least I had my memories with me. So, too, that you do not forget my memories either, they are one two three cot poem playing, four the memory of the repetitions, five the memory of the present, six the memory of what has not happened, seven the memory of messengers from the other side. Perhaps there is also eight, all the other memories as well, which are significant in one sense I suppose, but nothing insofar as they are just a heap of accidental encounters one after another.

So that is one two three four five six seven eight. Cot.

Poem. Playing. Repetition. Present. Notness. Others.
Accidents. Surely that is more than enough memories for
anyone. I aspire to nothing more. I have had a good life as
they say, and, as they say, what more could anybody want.
Except never to see or feel that black river that cannot
be crossed, but flows like a nothingness through the hole
of you. But I have never feared that black river, to my
detriment, except my lack of fear saved me at least from
kissing. Having had enough of life is not to say that it is
time that you will lose your hole and not live in the river
evermore. But one cannot think of this for ever without
madness, and so, after my experience had thrown my
organism into disarray for a while, off I went down the
road in the clothes of myself and my family that I had torn,
and in their jewellery too. Because I knew no one I

had nowhere to go but to go, and so, as things go, so I
went. I went with them wherever they would take me, and
at least I had my health. I went for a long time, but I talked
to no one, and lived nowhere, for the money that I had
was all for food, and I would not part with the jewellery.
For some reason, it had a grip on me, and would not allow
me to abandon it to another. At least it was spring, and I
was filled with the sense of things growing and pushing
through the soil, as they pulsed with life force, which is
so idiot and repulsive that it can only make you laugh.
It knows and sees nothing but push push push, until it
catches itself like a monkey that will not let go of the fruit
and so is stuck to the jar by its own desire. Life is like that
too, but even less allegorical as it were, because it is so
ubiquitous and less meaningful. Perhaps it is not even
deserving of the name life, being just the most familiar
kind of being. It's not as if anyone else has set a trap for
you. You are the trap you have set for yourself.

Yet I have seen beings of all kinds shed themselves until they are no longer themselves. Then what are they. Some wash away at that point into the black river. Others liquefy, and recompose themselves as something altogether different. Others hover in a state of suspended animation until they decide what it is that their desire would have them do. As I have been saying, some decide for kissing and some for poking and some for extra teeth and hair and some for other things. All decide. Then again, some decide not to be kissers or pokers or possessors, but mere animate pulsing flesh that gives off all the signs of life, but those alone, just all the signs. Nothing more. A decision that is no decision, to be nothing more than a refusal to decide. Nothing more. Not even nothing. Then again, the decision is taken without you because, as I say, the hilarious thing about this life force is that it really does not think, but still finds a way to catch itself in the trap that it itself is. Even though it is hilar-

-ious it is not very funny. At times it is sad and at others you have never seen anything so disgusting. There are more disgusting things than corpses. Some of those things are those things that pulse with nothing but bare life ignorant of the black river and the creatures of the other side and even of the things that do not happen for bare life is a sign as wrong as you like. There was much life such as this when I was on the street. It took on all manner of appearances. Bare life can be toothless, or it can go to the dentist, or it can scrabble along on all fours begging for mercy, or it can give orders as forcefully as an emperor. But no matter what these differences might be, bare life is bare life and as wrong as any sign can be.

At least this is what you discover when you live on the

street without parents, and must be husband and wife
and mother and father to yourself. On the street, you
meet many forms of life and hear many tales, although,
as I began by saying, you can never believe the tellers but
must find out just where their particular and specific lies
lie, in order to discern the truth of the tale. As everywhere,
kissers are the most common of peoples, and though I
hate them, they are not bad in themselves. Indeed, I must
even admit that nothing would happen without them, for
they are the glue of society. Society is based on kissing.
Sometimes even kissing can be more than glue, of which
more below, but still it stinks with the stench of something
putrefying as it grows. There were many kissers on the
street. Also, there were more pokers

than I had even imagined from my previous experience.
I liked the pokers as I said, because they could be radiant
as the sun. As you may have guessed, there are gradations
of poker. Some pokers poke for the better, others for the
worse. The pokers I preferred were those who did not poke
indiscriminately, but chose those they wished to poke with
such care that the spark of power that invariably erupted
from the first poke of the stick was rigorous and silent
as lightning. It could split the victim in two, as lightning
splits the night it illuminates. It is important to say that,
although people are truly divided into such categories as
kissers and pokers, there are such variations within these
categories that a good poker would be unrecognisable as
the same sort of creature as a bad, and, indeed, the effects
that the style of, say, a kisser has may be as different as a
crane and a snake, or as a big city and a hamlet that struts.

I had been on the streets for what felt like forever though
I was still young and had my good looks about me, though

when I say good looks I mean real looks, not just as a wrong sign taken for what does not happen. Though I had encountered and spoken with so many beings none had any hold over me, nor I over them, and though this may have seemed like freedom, I knew that something was not right, or rather that something was lacking that made freedom also lack. Whereupon I was ripe, as they say, or green, for such a fruit is always in and out of season at once, and there is no way to pluck it at the right time. It was then I encountered a person who was a wrong sign, but a wrong sign that bore no resemblance to the kissers or the pokers or the mouthers. Obversely, this sign bore a resemblance to them all, but without similarity. Or perhaps he was similar without resemblance. I am unsure which, but, in any case, it was still wrong, but anomalously so. To others I am sure they noticed not wrongness nor anomaly or indeed anything to write home about if indeed one had a home to write to, which, you will recall, I did not.

I must therefore say something about the most paradoxical of all the wrong signs that there are. For if as I say everyone is a wrong sign who does not know that they are wrong, or, if they do, are incapable of saying how they are wrong or what a right sign would be, and if some wrong signs sign themselves as wrong and are for that reason more truthful though that truth remains obscure, there is another type of wrong wrong sign that has not truth behind it nor anywhere else. That kind of wrong wrong sign is nothing but itself and indicates nothing and points nowhere else. It is a sign so superficial that it is exhausted just by being looked at. When you come across such a sign, it is truly a sign of transcendence, if only because it is so absolutely here that there is no other behind it. At first, I hoped that this wrong wrong sign had in some way escaped the black river. It is the rarest of all signs, and once you encounter such a sign, if only for an instant, you can never forget it. Even the gurgling of the black river will fade momentarily into nothingness. Perhaps I can say th-

-at this then would be my ninth memory after cot poem playing repetition present notness others accidents love. Yes, it is a big word and much abused and maligned as well it should be, but there is no other word for it, and there it is. The sign that signs itself as wrong so wrongly brings love in its encounter and is pure beauty. Well that is anyway how I felt about my friend, although I could never quite tell whether my friend was male or female or indeed anything definite, for though such things are obviously of the utmost importance, in this case it was, if not irrelevant, still a side issue which for some reason did not vitiate the quality of my love. I will not hide the fact here that we constantly put things in and out of each other's bodies that would have disgusted many, and indeed myself in any other comparable situation, but even the kissing that we did under such conditions did not resemble to me in my delirium the kissing in which others engaged. Then again I was at times disgusted but somehow the disgust was part of the strange flavour of the whole thing, and even the kissing and the disgust that I have tried since to regret I cannot. If

my friend was neither male nor female, or at least indeterminate, or something entirely other, I still could not help but think of that poem from childhood that my father had perhaps recited incorrectly and which I must repeat. I think it somehow important to the situation. She walks in beauty like a night of cloudy climes and starry skies and all that's best of dark and light meet in the aspects of her eyes.

Indeed, I would recite this poem to my loved one whether him or her or whatever, and we would look into each other's eyes, and he or she would see me as I was, and even if disgusted, this would not put him or her off, and I would look at his or her wrongness, and be amazed at its beauty. Indeed I was made so happy by its beauty that I forgot not only the sound of the black river racing, but even the pain of the spittle the ambassador had deposited in my ear. I even came to believe that that spittle might have run out onto the pillow one night as I slept, and drained away for good.

I must say that although there was certainly love at play and the wrong wrong sign made me very happy, it also made me very unhappy, and there was no way of communicating this to either the sign itself or to others, or indeed to myself, for after all I was in love. Unhappiness is part of love, real unhappiness, not just the dissatisfaction inevitably attendant upon brute existence, and without that unhappiness nothing at all. For the torments of love are certainly part of the essence or existence of love, and happiness and unhappiness are just the dust and shadows thrown up and scattered across the world by the fact of love. What could be said of this to anyone, indeed, as I have just said or at least implied, most of all myself. Love is not love that can its explanation find, though explanation is certainly what those in love can come to search for, as if their encounter was a fate and not any old accident in which two are thrown together like Ares and Aphrodite thrown together make Harmony. For Harmony is a dreadful thing insofar as one must suffer it, as the Dutch innkeeper imagined it, as a graveyard dedicated to perpetual peace. Yet it is the very antithesis of the grave. Well, the explanation escapes all, certainly the two, and certainly the others who cannot help but look on in stupefaction or complacent contempt and believe it perfectly comprehensible, for such a pair would surely find satisfaction with each other, or, on the contrary, perfectly incomprehensible, for what does he or she see in him or her. What is

that creature, such that that creature find love in the plugs and caverns of its universal stimulation and confusion, and not in that creature or that creature. Well, speculation is also at the heart of love, a speculation that is sometimes terror that will not turn its face, or sometimes unavowed repetition of ancient patterns that seize the one or the other with the great shadowy figures of dissimulating memory, or sometimes pure glory in a solipsism that wreaks havoc in the name of love. Though these are always possibilities that are present, or at least absent but effective, and, my goodness, why not affective, they are not sovereign here. They are not sovereign here, for nobody, not even the little bastard event of Eros that triggered the latch of the encounter in the first place, and has now found its claws painfully and unpleasantly caught in the wheels and pulleys of the unique mechanism that it could not help but trigger like a curious and naughty child. Well, innocence is one thing, but to be caught like a child without sovereign nor sovereignty, with only the other as company, leaving aside the wriggling irritation of little Eros trying desperately to detach himself from the cogs of the machine, well what is to be said but hard luck all round, all are for it now, and want and do not want that crushing and pressing as the irrevocable.

The creature I loved was the sign of signs. I knew that one does not have or hold such a sign, that it is not something that can be possessed or kept, for it is only there. Having said this, of course, and despite my knowing that you cannot have or hold such a sign, it was impossible not to fear its very openness to the air and the salt of the sea, and the demands of others such as kissers and pokers who are always around, and may in one way or another try to steal or damage the sign of signs for their own ends. For though pokers have always given me the light of the sun, in this case I was apprehensive that a poker would try to poke this wrong wrong sign, and that was something I could not even the thought of abide. All of which is very strange, for what does it mean that the very thing you love is the very thing that makes you angry for the reasons you love it. There is nothing you can do but fly into a rage and accuse the sign of treacheries and every defence that you can even imagine it making seems flawed and self-defeating.

Then all has become nothing but lies lies lies. So though you know better, you cannot help but lose it. For this is one of the signs that you are truly in love, that you betray yourself and the loved one and cannot help it. For you are not only in a passion, you are passion. Then there are tears and recriminations and if you are not careful you may fall into the ablative or supinate love that is the love of kissers, and though this seems like love, it is not. It is love's abdication and ruin. Any sign of signs, and every such sign, is not something to which you sacrifice, for it is not a god. Indeed, it may inhabit the furthest reaches of the universe from gods. It is simply something that happens to be an exhausted sign and to think it something to which you sacrifice is strangely enough the highest evil. Though many kissers would hold precisely the opposite, it is because they would wish to destroy its weakness out of their own. To sacrifice is to claim power over the deity to which you are sacrificing, though it seem the opposite. Power is not something you can have over love, although, on the other hand, it is precisely all it is too. So you often have power and love intertwined to the point of violence. That

I can say this at all is, of course, a lesson that one learns only too late, when it is not only a lesson in love, but a lesson about the sort of lies you tell to tell the truth without knowing one from the other, or even where they turn, for as you turn you lie. On the one side of the page is what you know to be virtue, and on the other side terror, but in fact the terror may be virtue and vice versa, for, as I never tire of saying, signs are all wrong signs. But what happens when the sign is wrong squared. You can never separate them for they are identical twins, although only one of them looks like itself, and it is impossible to say which one that is. There are always two sides of a page, but recto and verso or one and two is not easily discerned. Maybe page two begins halfway down the first page that comes after it. This is difficult to grasp, I understand, but, there you are, that is just how it is. In fact, it is even more difficult than this, for, if the love of the beauty of the wrong sign mixes virtue and terror in inextricable ways, then what is the difference between love and power. This question often occurred to me in the throes of love, when my loved one and I were placing objects in the other's body in disgusting ways. Some of them looked as I have said, like kissing, and some like poking, and some like possession, and some

mouthing.

We went on like this for some time, each putting objects of all kinds in the other's body in all kinds of ways, for

there is nothing like it in the world, given that there is,
some say, only one wrong wrong sign per person per life,
and what other kind of life is there. Yet somehow, after
some time, though there was no diminution of my love,
even, perhaps, an intensification to the point of unbearable
happiness, I was thrown into a misery that had not to do
with the wrong wrong sign per se but rather with being or
belonging with that sign, a situation which for some reason
became impossible to maintain. Or, at least, so I felt at the
time, if perhaps it was nothing at all, just a momentary itch
which might well have been overlooked if I had had the
patience or the equanimity. But overlooking the smallest
detail is exhausting when one is in love, as I am sure you
too have found, because love painstakingly assembles
all the detail as if building a house of matchsticks or
rather a hollow horse of matchsticks on which to ride. I
am really trying to say that, somehow, after some time, I
had to betray the wrong wrong sign. It was as if I was in
a madness and a frenzy and a depression that older and
wiser peoples may once have denominated the descent
of a god which seized me and for which, though I had no
control, I am nevertheless to blame. If a fate of a person
is not chosen or willed by them it is their fate. I'm sorry,
that's that, and that's just the way it is, and I have never
felt any the better about it as if fate was something about
which one so did. So,

although I was the one who abandoned the loved sign, I
still cannot stop myself from crying hysterically, neither
brave nor strong enough to assume the consequences of
a decision I never really wanted to make in the first place.
The very act was enough to break me, and it will be forever
impossible to forget as the light streamed down the ceiling
and coagulated in little droplets of horror about its mouth

and nose, those gaping Os that opened and closed onto the simple organic functioning of an animal interior while the sign itself, that invisible film that sheathed the technical automatism of the outside world from the roiling obscenity of the organism had been altogether abolished by my declaration of independence. Certainly, the abolition was only momentary, and the sign's return to self was legibly marked by the blossoming of pure aggression, but events recollected in the melancholy of tranquillity or tranquillity of melancholy testify only to the survival of the thing that sustains them, and surely in this instance that thing can only be and could have been none other than myself.

It is no consolation, rather an intensification of the horror, that I was unable to control the me that the sign of signs had transfigured, if only transitorily. Forever is the promise, but forever is not as optimistic as it may sound. It is something quite else. If I were now to recapitulate the sequence of my memories once more, or rather of my memory-types, as they are not always individual memories of particular situations and events, they would run cot poem play repetition present notness others accidents love, and of all of these love is by no means my fondest memory. Then again, if one thinks about it, memory is not exactly about fondness anyway, but rather the catastrophe of what's gone piling up behind you as you lurch backwards into a future you will never see. The future, a friend said, a poker I think he was, lasts a long time. That time is not a time to remember, although it is so long you would think by the end you might have learned something even though you have not. Only the retrospective future seems unavoidable, but retrospectively is just another memory of what you never had. The point is that, although love is not my fondest memory, not by a long shot, nor my oldest memory, as that is of the cot, it is perhaps my deepest memory. If deepest here can be taken to mean the one that is at once present and omnipresent, although it is a memory of times lost and therefore in a way omnipresent loss and therefore in a way not really there at all therefore in a way not really even a memory.

This loss is pain itself, pure pain, pain in its purity. Humans, though wrong signs, are so constituted as to feel such loss as pain, although it is just as true that they can find many ways of covering it up too. Such ways are always failures, for a loss cannot be destroyed. Anyway, I was, in the immediate aftermath of the loss, so disconsolate that I myself felt lost, and did not know what I had done although it had been, as I have said, I who had done it. For acting and knowing are, as you know, so often at odds. The meaning of an act is hidden from its actor, at least until that actor becomes a knower. Yet in becoming a knower, the knower is no longer the actor who acted, and so has not the force of the act, only its residue. The residue hangs around for you, though it was not you that did it. So you are always remembering things you have not done, though it is precisely you who did them.

Anyway, thinking about this also causes pain, so when I had done what I did though I knew not why I sat down disconsolate in the gutter where pain piled upon pain in a great tower or even a pagoda of des-

-pair. The pain in my ear from the ambassador's spittle had returned, and I conjectured that maybe the spittle had had something to do with this separation between acting and knowing that unbound and deranged me. I do not know for how long I sat there. Years maybe. While I was sitting

there disconsolate and conjecturing, I also took some time
to sob loudly for I have found that the emitting of certain
sounds under certain conditions can help a person to feel
less pain, or at least mitigate or curb the endless swelling
of pain. Of course, sometimes this is not quite the case,
as there are further examples in which such emissions of
sound fail quite soundly to do so. On the contrary, such
sounds can intensify the pain, and if that's what you like,
so be it. In any case, I was sitting disconsolate in the gutter
sobbing intermittently with great heaving sobs, so great
and heaving that any passer-by may have been forgiven
for thinking I had contracted a fatal respiratory disease
whereof I was in the final throes thereof. For my chest
was heaving like the belly of a dying animal, and throttled
whooping sounds were issuing from my throat like they
were the whoops of imminent expiration.

I sat there whooping for some time until it grew nearly
dark, and the stars were almost out, and there was perhaps
a moon in the sky. I was still whooping in that noteworthy
fashion when a strange man passed by, and took an
interest in my story. It turned out to be the case that he
was a powerful man, although you would never know it to
look at him, quite the contrary. He was interested in love
too, although you would also never know it to look at him.
His real interest was what you might call power, although,
as I have said, the distances between love and power are
often negligible, and indeed love and power are like the
two ends of a piano-accordion, sometimes near, sometimes
far, but never not connected by a crinkled bladder.

The man was not large in physical terms, but the signs
he made were ferocious as I had ever seen, though, as I
have perhaps said or at least implied, there were many

ferocious signs to be encountered on the street. But he was the most real in terms of the understanding of signs that I had ever seen, insofar as he understood all to be wrong and false. Even the ambassador who had examined me so thoroughly had not been so at one with the real of signs, for he pretended at least to be working for the government and, as a representative, had still to permit kissing and poking and all the many other rituals that are incumbent upon such representatives to permit. This man was so real, he had no patience for any rituals, no matter how innocuous or cunningly disguised, and saw straight through to whether his interlocutor was a kisser or a poker or whatever. He was in this sense like me aware of the real world that nobody else can abide, from which they flee into various postures of denial. Unlike me, he wanted above all to become master of the real world as he found it. There was nothing that he was scared of in the world, because he knew exactly what each was capable of as soon as he had clapped eyes upon him or her. Except

I might say he was fearful of me, because he knew that I too saw what he saw, or at least we both saw wrong signs as just the ways things are. He was fearful of me not because we both saw the way things are, but because I saw and did not want to be the master of real things. I wanted only love. What else he saw in me, I do not know. As I have said, that is impossible entirely to know. It is clear that he did see something more in me. He saw immediately that I had the spit of the ambassador within me, and said that that was a bad and sorry thing, but that there was now nothing anyone could do, and that I would until the end of time feel that spittle coming alive every now and again in my head and burning. I had been marked badly he said, and he could not fix that mark which had marked itself in the real but had not killed me. Indeed, the spittle was now a talisman to serve and protect, although, like everything else that comes so to serve, it had to have a cost. Yet there was something else that troubled him, and even though he had no fear of anyone, he had a fear of me. But his fear

was not something he denied, and so he asked whether I would like to come and work with him. He said, laughing, that he was a good man to work with, as he always obeyed the rules as long as they suited him, and at least he knew what rules were. He added that he understood that I was sad because my friend had gone, and that he would let me hold onto my sadness, though no others would permit such a thing. People are terrified of sadness, he said, because it demolishes the foundations of what never took place. Love, he said, for I presume that is what you had, or were in, or however you prefer to talk about it, is not something the world can permit, because it is of the real world. They can only bear it by making love an image, and, as image, it can come and go as it pleases, and that is acceptable. But I, as you know, am a man of the real world, and so I must acknowledge that it is real, if the opposite of what I know. For as you know, I am a master of fear and not a man of love.

As I am a magistrate or master of fear he said, my business is altogether with the triggers and levers that set humankind off on their various ways as kissers and pokers and mouthers and possessed, and it is important to know how best they are to work together for your own ends. Not only must you know the triggers and levers, but if you set one off at the wrong time then O well you must be prepared to suffer the consequences of your mistake. They can be dreadful, the consequences. Often it is harder still. Even if you set one off at the right time you have to consider whether it might thereby interfere with another whose time is not yet quite right, and that one might then in turn make everyone suffer dreadful consequences. If you wish to tamper with one human thing and its triggers and levers, well, you must be prepared to think of every human thing at the same time, and this is a very complicated and risky procedure, for one small miscalculation, boom, that's it. In

to the bargain you must remember that if you wish to be a master of fear there are others who wish the same thing, and you must always be mindful of what they can do because you may not even know who they are, and, worse still, they may not even know who they are, being like everyone deluded about their being. You must watch very closely, and not mistake a kisser for a poker, or a possessed being for a master of fear, or vice versa. The risks are great, certainly, but no greater in a particular sense than the risks of being in love, eh young person, for the consequences of love gone awry are great, are they not. Then he laughed speaking of love, which, by his own admission, he neither knew nor understood, but understood that love and power are in some secret way one and the same, though they are equally absolutely opposed without reconciliation only antagonism for ever. Yet antagonism, as he at once pointed out, is something that he understood very well.

Antagonism, he said, or control over the real bodies of wrong signs, not only means antagonism between us and them, between masters who may not be the masters who seem to be such. Nor is it simply between the groups that they control, or control over the triggers and levers of the aforementioned. No, control is gained by splitting the groups of each master within. For each master is concerned to foster antagonism amongst those beings that are his subjects. He instils fear, because antagonism between and within offers the greatest leverage. If you are a master of fear, this is what you are best at, and then nothing can stand in your way. Except for other masters, of course, but that is part of the job description. Only the thing that forever escapes control is control over love, for love sends bodies into that frenzy which is hardest of all to control, as it runs parallel to the black river without crossing it or falling in, although love is also easiest of all to control for the same reason.

At the mention of the black river, my ears pricked up, and the master or magistrate looked upon me and knew that I knew, but somehow he also knew that the spittle that the ambassador had deposited within was burning. At which he smiled. Ah, that man the ambassador, he said, he is a true master, and yet I think I could tell him a thing or two. He paused reflectively, and said that even with those whose triggers and levers are safe in your hands you can lose control. Then your minions might revolt despite themselves, and despite all good care being taken over the wherefores and witnesses, fear will turn into rebellion and insurrection and before you know it you are in the oven with the other victims yourself. Perhaps

he said, that will happen to me one day, though I am the greatest master in this locale, excepting the ambassador, though his powers are not his alone, but are also those of inertia and indecision, though those too are powers, and that constrains him. For fear is really just a name for many different kinds of power and we, he meant himself and the ambassador, have very little in common though we both are masters. We have never spoken directly to one another as of yet, but perhaps one day we shall see.

These things, he continued, must in any case remain mysterious, as mysterious to the powers that act as to the material that is enacted, and, well, it is an interesting problem I suppose, one that you may perhaps be interested in thinking about as I can see you are a thinker, at least of a kind. How, after all, can a magistrate act through the mere power of a magic word that pulls the triggers and the levers and thereby turns the diverse loose collocation of kissers and pokers and mothers at his disposal into the existence of a well-oiled machine that clanks and whirrs and produces product when and as he sees fit. Well, I have always thought that my group is I, and I am the multitudes at my own disposal, and there is no mystery because I am a master. Yet, as a master, I must always act as if I never reflected. Reflection is the domain of mirrors and images, but a master is a master of the mirror's tain, and the force of images that make reflection possible without being able to be seen within it.

Anyway, he said, you must now come with me, because I can use you to my profit, and you me, and we will know power together as you never believed. He took my hand and led me from the street where I had sobbed now for so long and to the compound where the builders lived. In the stream of events that do not happen, but which people take however to be the real world, he was a builder among builders. He built big factories for humans who were very rich or with the government. At his command was an army of builders, comprised of course, as indeed is every group, of kissers and pokers and mouthers and possessed and so on, but, as they built for their occupation, they were called builders. The magistrate knew as I have said that to spurn is to spur, and that the threshold of power is the threshing ground where creatures are thrashed, and so he spurned and threshed and thrashed with a joy that is the joy that magistrates have always experienced before the pointless suffering and pain of men and piles of bodies and oh what joy it is.

The magistrate was so fond of the pain and piles that he would often build upon the pain, and when I say build I mean build. You would be surprised no matter how much a man or woman of the world you fancy yourself to be if you really knew just how many buildings are not built on steel and concrete, but on the bodies of persons of all varieties. The magistrate liked to throw them in and watch as they squeaked and squealed and struggled uselessly in the pit before helping them under with his little shovel, with which he would shovel them slowly under. They would see him smiling, and his strong smiling hands as the soil fell, and sometimes hear his laughter, and, sometimes when other builders were present, they too would lend a hand and pitch in, as they say, all laughing and chattering, sometimes mocking the victim who would struggle and fulminate against the inevitable as he or she was shovelled under to rest as they say, now rest forever under a compacted crown of earth, and maybe just live long enough to feel it being stamped down, the earth in the mouth and the final gag and swallow.

I remained there for many years and sat beside the magistrate who had lifted me from the gutter and who was a powerful man with his minions in every basement and alleyway and office and boardroom and even in the foundations. With him I prospered. I thought often of my memories, particularly of my lost love, which continued to cause me great pain. I nevertheless kept my memories and feelings secret and intact, as sometimes the communication of pain caused by a loss will vitiate the force of that pain, and, thereby, by some supra-rational logic of causality the power of the loss itself, which is what I clearly did not want. I ate well and was treated as, if not an equal by the magistrate, at least as someone worthy of respect and as a free person. It went like this. I was happy as could be, which is not to say I was happy, only happy as could be, which was in fact not that much because could is not a big word and can become anything in the mouth of anyone. But

nonetheless I stayed, and even came to love the shovelling under, as there is something very singular about the moment of a person's death. For a while I was almost convinced that kissers died in their own way, as did pokers, and so on, and I would lean forward intently straining so as not to miss the smallest twitch or groan from the dying object of my attentions, so as to see if the instant of death had its styles and genres. Indeed, I can conclusively state that it does, although, despite my hope and my hypotheses, they were not the ones I thought. Some of them snivelled and some raged and some were silent and some begged for mercy and others did not, and yet if you looked carefully at their faces or indeed at other parts of their anatomies, which were sometimes buried after their faces, especially when the magistrate was in a particular mood, and would have his victims buried head first in lime or face down or disembowelled before interment, the expression and the mood often did not match each other. In other words a sniveller would appear strangely calm, and though his or her lips would be mouthing the most frightful of ab-

-negations, they otherwise betrayed an unthinkable satisfaction, or a man proudly raging would tremble with ripples of terror and childishness, or silent ones would look quite sad as if they pitied their killers, or all of these could be mixed up with one another in every imaginable variation of posture and emotion and expression. I was often dizzied by the magnificence and variety of the moods of death, and even in those who had lived as kissers or as possessed, and sometimes even the glum undead bodies of those bare lives I have spoken of, would thrill with an unexpected if instantaneous vitality at the moment of their murder, as if the brutal extinction of their life was a glorious apotheosis. Anyway, as I said, I stayed with the magistrate and his builders for many years, and the entire time the magistrate grew in power and stature as around him swelled the aura of death. This is however something about which no one would speak, not only because they feared for their own lives, but because, as the magistrate himself mused, a major power of power is that it prevents the truth from being told about itself, even by those who have nothing to fear nor gain, as if something essential was being shared in such misprisions, whether deliberate or unconscious. But

all good things must come to an end as they say, and in time even the magistrate was forced to look at himself in the mirror and admit that age was upon him as it was not upon his victims, and there were now also labour laws that prevented his continued work in the building industry, for no one likes to see old men twitching along with their trolleys and their barrows loaded down with earth and bricks. So off you go, said the laws that had until then sustained him in his flaunting or rather flouting of them. Like, ah, all good things remarked the magistrate, I too must go, though I shall not go far, for though we bury people alive we do not disrespect the law, and indeed one day I still hope to lean over at a dinner wearing a bow tie and whisper into the ear of the ambassador things that would shock him and make him blush with shame.

The magistrate my friend, who was going, who was frightful, who knew things he could tell the ambassador, was to have a party to farewell him to his next state of life, whatever that would be. So the builders hired at great expense a fabulous boat for his party, and we were all to sail out of the harbour and into the sea for the whole night. From the boat at sea at night the city would be lit up along the coast like a bonfire or like the city of god where angels sing continuously his praises and I and the builders would toast each other all evening and praise each other and the going man as if the city really belonged to us with all its fires and signs. So the kissers and the pokers and the various other builders and he and I went out together one night on the open sea where one could see the foam on the waves like the spit that kissers leave between your toes, and we toasted each other in the pitchness of the dark with the city illuminated behind.

I was very happy, and had almost forgotten the wrong wrong sign with which I was still in love although it was over, and it seemed too that everyone else was likewise as happy, staring at the sea and the foam on the sea like the spittle of kissers and the lights of the city like an army of pokers were poking all over the dark of the hills and all the possessed were working as one for to bring me rare delicate berries from the forests of the dark hills or game from the distant flatlands beyond the hills which could not even be seen. But such happiness cannot last, and, indeed, is invariably the prelude or entrée to some great misfortune as you have witnessed in regard to the story of my calamities, and one might even suspect that the role of happiness is simply as a foil to the main course which is that of misery, and happiness is there only to make the taste of misery all the more bitter and painful. Not that that is a bad thing, of course, for pain and misery are the substance of freedom, and without them nothing, nothing at all. Yet pain and misery are very unpleasant indeed by definition, and often their unpleasantness has much to do with their unexpectedness, so when

one would have least expected it the revellers on the boat turned as one and seized the magistrate whose success they had until that moment been celebrating, or, as it now appeared, only appeared to be celebrating. What are you doing, he cried immediately, but his cry was simply a cry for, as a great magistrate, he already knew, though he would surely be kicking himself for not noticing before if he were still around to be kicking himself that is. We have had enough, they cried in return, you have taken advantage long enough, and now you are going you are sure to be gone. Then the magistrate laughed in his turn, bitterly as it was, for it was clear to him that they were only able to kill him when he was already in a manner of speaking gone. You are killing me for failing to remain your master, he said, not for having been your master. This utterance threw them into confusion or rather angered them further, which often comes to the same thing. They began to bind him with packing tape and they wound and wound until he was just a bundle of brown plastic bonds except for a strip around his eyes and then they opened the boat's furnace door and his eyes widened and they threw him in just like that and with a certain satisfaction. Some clapped their hands as if saying by that gesture, well, a good day's work, and others just smacked their lips as if they had eaten a tasty dish,

which they hadn't, although the stench that the magistrate made as he burned was really like meat of any kind roasting away in the oven and if you had not seen it with your own eyes you might almost believe that the boat was just a holiday boat and the revellers were cooking their meat and potatoes and vegetables and were about to settle down to a slap-up meal and smear their faces with the grease of a slaughtered tasty animal and celebrate some festival perhaps a birthday or mother's day or a religious feast of some order. Before the door of that oven I thought naturally of the miracles that are said to be dispensed by the gods, and for a brief instant imagined the magistrate to be kept unharmed. He would then, at a propitious moment, simply knock once on the door for it to spring open and he would exit and subdue his enemies, that is, his erstwhile subjects with an arm guided by the divine. But instead all there were were his screams as he burnt, and every now and again the popping of what I imagined to be his flesh popping in the heat of that final furnace.

When they had popped my friend the magistrate in the oven, and everyone was happy with the stench of burning flesh, and the screams that he made as he burned were still echoing over the night waves, the conspirators turned to me and then to one another as they knew they had to silence me somehow because I was not really one of them. Perhaps if I disappeared into the oven with the magistrate they could pretend to the inquiry that it really had been a terrible night of grisly accidents insofar as two people had fallen overboard and to the further misery of their widows their bodies were never recovered, although of course I was not myself married. And I thought that this was to be my fate and I immediately thought of my dead friend the magistrate but also of the love I had betrayed and then of my other memories cot poem playing repetition present notness others accidents and they all flashed before me as a life is said to do before itself as it terminates, which is to say that it ends, ends absolutely as far as others are concerned, but for itself it never ends, just cycles to the point of termination whereupon it recycles forever, having the eternal flashing back without any escape into death.

My flashing back was interrupted by the builders, who had decided that I was not to die. They had agreed upon a more suitable way of disposing of me, without further dirtying their hands. Their hands were already very dirty, as I'm sure you will understand, and not just from the burning. They trussed me up instead in what was left of the roll of packing tape with which they had bound the magistrate before throwing him into the oven, and propped me as if I were some kind of log against the closed door of the oven which was still very hot. The tape began to melt, so they laid me down on the rolling deck of the boat so I could see the spray of stars so distant and so indifferent above and clustered over me smirking. We will take you to the factory, they said, smirking, for there you will have a good job, and it will all be legally above board, and no one will ask questions, and in any case we are men and women of conscience and we do not need your death weighing further upon that conscience, for, since your death is irrelevant, it may weigh all the more heavily. I thought they had never heard of the aphorism if your conscience offend thee flush it out, but did not think it the best moment to apprise them of it as they had just burnt the magistrate alive and it did not seem that they were asking for my thoughts. Indeed

they were not, for one of them began to hit me on the head with my own shovel and eventually I passed out although it took some time and maybe they wished it to do so so as to cause me much pain, which it did. Finally, I blacked out as they say. I awoke in such a strange place it is difficult to describe, not because it is really difficult to describe, but because it was not a place that you could believe could exist, although I assure you it certainly did. I was in an enormous room larger than I had ever been in before. It was a dappled white, lit by artificial lights. None of which is strange, admittedly, but what is strange is that the room had neither windows nor doors and there was no way that I could tell how I was ever introduced there. As far as I could ever tell there were not even secret windows or doors and I could never find a soul who would tell me differently. But contrary to your expectations perhaps I was not dead and neither was I dreaming and I tell you now that there do exist rooms without windows or doors and people if people is the word for it do live in such rooms, if living is the

word for it in such rooms as these. And though I pondered it often, I never discovered how I had been deposited in that room, though I have my theories as you may later hear. As I slowly got my bearings I realised that my head was still bleeding from the wound that I had been given by the killers of the magistrate on the boat and, although I will not mention it again, the wound did not heal but bled constantly for the remainder of the time that I was there. It was healed in the circumstances that I will come to mention later but, as I said, I will not mention it again as there are more important events to relate. The enormous room was filled with rows of desks. There were so many desks that I could not believe that so many could fit into a single room, but that is how it was. At each of these desks a woman was chained and, much like myself, each of the women was bleeding often profusely from the head. I was not chained for some unfathomable reason, but was free to wander up and down at will, though there was essentially nowhere else to go and things as you can imagine did not change very much. At one end of the enormous

room as I later discovered were a row of different sorts of creatures who I will call the coordinators, who sat and scratched at each other with their weird antennae which were wild with colours and very repulsive to behold. They did nothing but scratch scratch scratch and whistle at each other in an incomprehensible fashion, for they did not seem to comprehend everyday speech though I tried often to communicate with them. Sometimes they would use words like any other person, but when you tried to comprehend it, the words did not quite make sense. And those were the two kinds of creatures in the enormous room which, if it bore any resemblance to anything, was like some kind of enigmatic factory in which strange work went on. The work of course never left the room as there was no way that it could. There was one other creature that lived in the factory, which was neither like the coordinators nor the bleeding women at their desks but seemed to be some sort of go-between. I must describe her at length for I had never seen anything like it, though by that time I had as you should have realised experienced rather much.

The name of the creature was devil arse because not only

was she a stick of hate that quivered and quivered with a fury and an unhappiness she was able to express only as the wrongest of signs, but because she had an extra face on her rump which made it difficult to sit down because sitting down would squash that face. The face was in any case horribly deformed and squashed because she could not help but sit down and lie occasionally, for she, for some reason, felt she had to pretend when in the company of others that she did not have that extra face. But she did and you could often hear it squawking gently when she was sitting there, a smile on her front face like she was not a stick of hate and as if where her buttocks should have been there was not her other face. The paradox, if paradox you could call it, was that the other face was the face of a sort of joy that wished only to sing as free as the birds as they say, as free as the birds if it had not been the face on the arse of devil arse. But it was and the years had not been kind to that poor face which was now as I say squashed and splattered like a ripe fruit, say an apricot had dropped from the trees and onto the hard ground only to be picked apart by the very birds that it had wished to sing like. Well that was what that other face was like, the residues of squashed unfulfilled joy. But her front face was always smiling because smiling was what she had been taught by the women when she was a little girl and now that smile could never come off though it was the biggest of all the lies which the women had taught her, though the women had also taught her that to sin is a lie and god sees all our lies. So devil arse knew she was sinning because she had no pride in the joy that her arse face sang of and she sat on it until she realised that, though she was squashing her arse face, that arse face was part of her and it hurt to squash it. So she was bitter all the time and hateful and could not do the thing that would have saved her from herself, which was to embrace her arse face as a part of her and then she would have felt such joy. But she could not and because she could not it impelled her into incessant or rather I should say relentless movement for she had become a scavenger in the vast factory hall with all the other women who were just tired and nothing but and sat and sat and worked until they bled with the effort. And because they bled as they worked they were too tired to do anything but submit when devil arse scuttled over and dribbled her bilious and insidious slime over what they were doing so they no longer wanted it but had to. And devil arse would treat them as if they were mewling infants and pat them on their scalps which were soft and sticky with the blood and even in parts the brain was showing through the scalp and then she would leave them with the slime that she carefully dribbled onto their work and take off with the good part. The good part she would write her name all over on every part

until there was nothing but her name devil arse devil arse devil arse all over it. Then she would take that stolen scrap which she had not made along the rows of women working and they could see her squashed arse face through her pants writhing and contorting its squashed features but helpless and unable to utter any real articulated sounds just an oooooooh and an aaaaaaah and devil arse would proudly carry the scrap which bore nothing but the words devil arse devil arse devil arse and take that scrap to the desk of the coordinators who sat and scribbled at the head of the factory overlooking the rows of women. And the coordinators were all thin and dry little sexless creatures like bugs who had strained themselves for years and years until they were only capable of feeding on the oleaginous residues of whatever the work was that devil arse had stolen from the bleeding women. They would take the scrap that devil arse gave them and with their little mandibles and claws would slowly nibble away at the legend devil arse devil arse until it was all gone. While they were feeding devil arse would slobber and bob with happiness at their desiccated eagerness and when they were done they would whisper good work good work at her and she would kowtow her way away again down the aisles

of bleeding women to filch another scrap on which to write her name. Although I was imprisoned there, in much the same boat as the women and devil arse and indeed the coordinators themselves, for some reason I had not been chained up like the bleeding women and was free not to leave but to wander the aisles in the same way as devil arse was free. Devil arse and I took an immediate dislike to each other, and foamed and bit if we ever happened to encounter each other in one of the aisles. Though I would not if I chose approach her, her dislike of me was such that she could not stay away and she took to hiding herself behind the benches waiting for me to walk by. Then she would leap out at me, her mobile and deceitful front face grinning and foaming and trying to gnaw me with her many teeth. I would have said at least she was not kissing me, but that was one of the worst things about devil arse because she did not just pat and steal and dribble but she would try to kiss as she did

so. I did not know what to do because she was favoured by the coordinators and was the one to bring them the scraps on which they fed because they never once left their desks but did whatever they did there while waiting for devil arse to deposit their next feed. I was trapped in the factory for some time, which was one of the most horrible places, but at the same time queerly comfortable for there were always scraps to eat and all I had to do was wander up and down and every now and then be seen to bleed a little with the women. One night I was sleeping fitfully by the feet of a bleeding woman when I did not exactly awaken but found myself in that state between waking and sleep and heard the black river's roar and heard the buzzing of the creatures of the other side approach and the milky darkness swelled within me and I knew what I was to do. So I a-

-rose and sought out devil arse who was still relentlessly stalking the hall though many of the bleeding women had collapsed into unconsciousness and in some cases bits of their brains were leaking out onto the desks and onto the work they had been doing until they had simply dropped. Devil arse leapt at me grinning with all her teeth and I let her very close to me, then gripped her by her lower teeth and, before she could shut her trap tight on my hand or dribble slime onto my personage, I tore off her lower jaw and hurled it across the hall where it made a horrible dull thudding sound as it landed. And devil arse screamed, a horrible high scream from her throat, and, between the thud of her lower jaw on the concrete and the horrible high scream from her throat, the noise gripped everyone in the hall in a pincer movement that bit into them like the piercing claws of a crab. And then

I saw something that I had never seen before. The coordinators streamed over their desks and scuttled towards me whistling like the steely whistling of a boiling kettle while the bleeding women rattled their chains and howled and I admit that I was scared in a way that I had never been scared on the street or in love or when I was just a false builder to be slaughtered. I had not even realised that the coordinators were able to leave their desks, for they had never done so the whole time that I had been there but had waited always in anticipation of devil arse bringing them their victuals. And devil arse flopped about, still straining to kiss me with what was left of her front mouth and throat that was also still shrieking, but I evaded her and ran, though, as I say, the place had neither windows nor door and there was nowhere to run. The coordinators were still coming for me and the whistling they made was terrible and, because I knew nothing about their powers, I could not know what they had in mind for me, though of course

it was clear they willed me no good and did not see my mutilation of devil arse as something that could remain unpunished and of course it could not. As they swarmed over me whistling I felt sure that this time I was dead and that the black river would rise in me and never sink again. But as each of the coordinators swung at me with a mandible or a claw their whistling ran away down their own limbs and into my body just as that poker from my childhood had expended his sunlight trying to poke me and my body thrilled in ecstasy as the coordinators swung and swung as if automatically. If a blow connected it was the coordinator not I that went down as if its life force had suddenly been sucked out and run into my body and I would feel a corresponding thrill of ecstasy as if its life force had somehow become mine or transferred to me and all my cells hummed like I was a machine that had been oiled and was happy to be running. They kept coming

and coming in waves until there were more bodies than
I remember coordinators and their corpses piled high to
the roof of the hall. And while this was going on, all the
bleeding women had awoken and were hooting and crying
and slamming themselves against their desks and rattling
their chains until they bled even more than usual and the
floor of the hall was ankle deep in their blood and it was
impossible to tell if we were in heaven or in hell. Devil

arse was slipping and sliding and screaming in the blood,
scrabbling for purchase in the hellish slick, when she
slid into one of the tables where a woman was chained.
And perhaps it was because the coordinators were dead
or mostly dead or, I would rather say, that they had been
waiting for just such an opportunity of mayhem and
disarray, the ladies all arose as one and broke their chains
as if they, the chains that is, had been nothing but illusory
figments of the place. They descended on devil arse as the
furies of old are said to have descended on their victims,
and, very quickly, there was nothing recognisable left of
devil arse, not even skin or nails or even a scrap of her
squashed rear face. Although the frenzy continued for
some time after that, finally I and the others realised that
the coordinators and devil arse were dead and that

escape was the next move that we should make if it were
possible and if indeed we wanted to escape, for it seemed
that among the bleeding women there were those who,
as it were, had spontaneously burst into existence at their
table with their chain and their head already gashed and
opened to the air that is their wounds open for devil arse
to poke and prod so they would work though they were
too exhausted for words. And where were those women to
go and what were they to do who had never done anything

but bleed and suffer at their tables making whatever it was they had been under pain of pain to make for the masters with their antennae and mandibles. So we all stood around trying to communicate, for as it happened many of the women had never learned to speak. Speaking was not required by their job, as only crying was required of them by the coordinators, and a bit of bleeding and some making too. It

was difficult also because the only language they understood was devil arse prodding them in their brains every now and again, and so, despite their hatred, they were clearly also mourning devil arse and could not bring themselves to celebrate as it should have seemed that they should have done. In any case, it was difficult to see what there was to celebrate since there was no way in or out of the factory and now they were not being forced to work there was nothing to eat too. For a number of days we all just sat around together starving and mourning the good old days of devil arse and even I began to miss the horrible contortions of her squashed rear face through her tight trousers as she weaved her way through the tables stealing scraps on which to write. Yet as we starved and became thinner and thinner, I believe, from the strange motions of the women's features and bodies, that they as well as I began to suffer strange visions that came as if from another place, and in my case it was the creatures who came from the other side of the black river which is what you would expect, I suppose, though I cannot verify if this was equally the case for the women who may have had other sorts of visitation.

The creatures from the other side surrounded me with their buzzing innards and made me listen to the voices of the rotting dead that filled them. Although the rotting dead spoke mostly of kissing in their own old strange ways, this time there were three voices that stood out among the swarm and they were the voices of my father and mother which were now, for some reason, one voice only, though I understood why this was very well, and another voice was that of the wrong wrong sign with whom I had been in love before my betrayal, and the third was that of my friend the magistrate of fear who had been burnt alive on the boat. Their voices were not only memories in themselves but, as memories, they called to me to remember my memories my memories alone cot poem playing repetition present notness others accidents love. Remember remember, they called, your memories are indestructible until you come to the black river, and even then the black river is the font and force of all you know. You will rot with us then, you will be rot, rot will be all.

At that my eyes rolled back into my head, yet I could somehow see with the whites of my eyes, and I stood up and announced to the women who had one and all seen the change come over me that we were to leave this building without doors together at once. Though as I said many did not know language other than the prodding of the bleeding brain by devil arse who was now dead, they all seemed to understand and set up an ululation. The ululating of the bleeding women set off the spittle of the ambassador in my ear, but, as their moaning grew in volume, even the walls which evidently had been patched so many times with paint that they were stippled and uneven even though white had been laid over white and so on and on over the uncountable years for which the factory had been in operation, even the walls began to tremble beyond the mere layering of paint. As the ululations swelled like the chattering of vast cicadas, the paint began to peel from the walls in great flakes like the crest of waves that crash incessantly upon the rocks of distant shores until those rocks are crushed and crushed to sand. The

flakes of paint as they fell hit the desks and floors and shattered like waves crashing upon rocks. They threw great sprays of dust of immemorial white paint upon us, the bleeding women and I, and, because of the blood on the women, the paint stuck to them until they were completely covered in coats of white paint like they were animated archaic statues from a great museum or as if they had emerged from a pooling of crusty albino blood. As every wave of paint crashed upon them the women's voices swelled even more, though they were already so loud that that seemed impossible, and paint crashed down faster and faster until it seemed the very sky was falling, and the air was filled with the crash of the heavens. I could see nothing through the mist of flakes. I could hardly breathe as the paint clogged my mouth and nose but could hear the women ululating about me and felt them cluster about me and the pain in my ear from the spit of the ambassador grew as their voices grew until my whole body had become a sort of resonating vessel for the two pains one of the spittle two of the voices and these two pains were so intense and antagonistic that I thought or rather felt that I was to die.

As my pains fought each other on the white field of my body they began to intermingle and form new relationships until there were no longer only two but a multitude of new pains. In the very movement by which the two split they split again but did not decrease in intensity with the splitting but on the contrary increased all shall we say qualitatively and as I just said I felt there was no question I was to die. Yet at every point where I thought I must have reached my limit there came another point after that and then another after that and I wished to be dead but there seemed that there would be no escape into death. And because it was impossible to see, it was like being held out into the nothingness of the blank void from which the only evidence that something existed outside of myself was the choir, the choir of women's voices around me which, though causing me pain, was not its reason or its

end. It was as though I had entered a timeless state of singing white pain, when there was an almighty cracking sound as if all had come unhinged and all of a sudden the cosmos lit up with an unearthly luminescence and at that very moment the women's ululation stopped and the pain stopped and for however long it was there was just this weird light enwrapping the white void and I and the women in our silent blindness. Then the storm of paint began to settle and clear and it became apparent that the walls had indeed come down and I and the women who now looked so like marble statuary that our group seemed to compose a scene from an elevated antique temple overlooking the sea were standing in the midst of the ruins of the factory in the blue heat of a summer's day. There were no clouds in the sky. There were other factories around us. On the road, the traffic had stopped and many people had stopped too, and all were looking at us as if at a tableau vivant or a nature morte and, moreover, as if they could not decide

whether we were flesh or fish or fowl or ash. For we were like, as I say, a strange collocation of statuary and indeed

even my eyes were still rolled back in their sockets,
showing only their whites so called although of course the
whites were traversed by a delicate tracery of red lines but,
whatever you call it, it was still the case that somehow I
could see though my pupils were rolled back into my head
and staring presumably at least toward the back of my
skull, that is, into my brain. So there we were all in white
and when the walls of the factory without windows or
doors came down the women and I were exposed to the
light of day again, although, as I say, it was surely the first
time that some of those women had ever seen the sun. And
everyone was staring at us as if they were witnessing some
strange scene from a film about times that were gone and
would never come again, that is, with a dreamy nostalgia
and slight boredom, when some

thing in me made a slight sound that was a sound that
could not have come from anywhere and all of the women
who had been still as statues jerked into movement
again without sound, and we began to move as one-yet-
many towards the nearest spectators who broke into
spontaneous applause as if they had been witnessing a
magnificent troupe of dancers, or were at the theatre, or
the opera, or indeed any similar kind of performance,
though they were also patently disturbed by our emergence
from the broken shell of a building like a monstrous
butterfly from a chrysalis in which it, as a caterpillar,
had liquefied to reform. As we swept towards them
they clapped louder and louder as if we were the most
entertaining experience that they had ever experienced or
as if they had been seized by a god in a sweat that would
not cool. But it was easy to hear in their applause that they
were fearful, as fearful as it is possible to be, but, at the
same time, rooted to the spot with their excitement at the

incredible spectacle we were providing,

as if we were simply a machine for entertainment and not
creatures that had been released from a factory with no
windows or doors. We swept closer and closer to them
in involuntary patterns without sound that were yet so
intricate that it would be impossible for an observer no
matter how cynical to believe that such a pattern had
simply occurred without calculation or at least a great
deal of practice, although that was indeed what happened
or indeed was happening. Then I realised that the
patterns we, that is, I and the women, were making as we
swept across the rubble were like those of a machine for
entertainment which casts shall we say a shine over those
it entertains until they no longer know why or what they
are doing, just lost enmeshed thoughtless in the infinite
complexity of its patterns and suffused with all the many
affects of captivation. Mingled as I say with this captivation
however is a terrible fear for

after all a machine for entertainment is also a cannibal
machine and although people will laugh and sing and cry
in the shine that it offers those feelings will never last as
even perfection cannot stand too much repetition. So each
machine has its shelf- or rather performance-life and then
that's it it must be carved up and its working elements
reassigned if possible to a different organization of artificial
moving parts that will in its turn suffer the same fate
which is after all the best of all possible fates for a cannibal
machine as opposed to its simply creating boredom
or indifference or falling into a big pit or whatever.
But though the machine's end is solely entertainment
or maybe also feeding on its own antecedents there is
always something mutant and terrifying about a cannibal

machine, first because of the fact I've just told you, that is, that it is made of the parts of others, some of which have been expressly chopped up for the purpose and it is both made from and feeds upon the parts of the others that comprise it and, second, because sometimes the cannibal machine somehow introduces the pure shine of its end which is nothing natural into the world, which is not a world of shine, and then, as they say, all hell breaks loose and many people die in all manner of disturbing posture just for that fleck of shine and this possibility is always a possibility for that shine is what people live off and for and through though they know it to be

false. For sometimes cannibal machines lose control or, perhaps, those they are constructed to entertain lose control, over the machines or perhaps over themselves, and, instead of chewing up the other machines on which they feed to put out their momentary shine, they begin to chew up the people for which they shine and that shine bathes those it gobbles, that is, its new devotees in its unearthly glow and they cannot help but wish it to last forever for that shine opens up new possibilities hitherto undreamed of in their philosophy and they cannot bear that those possibilities be mere entertainment, so insist they must be made real and there you go the cannibal machine starts to gobble the world for which its job was only to shine on briefly and as the world goes so does the very shine which was to be introduced to it and the shine itself turns into foul matter that pretends itself still to shine. And this was precisely what was happening to us for as we brushed our captivated applauding audience they burst immediately into flame and burnt away with unbelievable rapidity without a trace other than a hint of greasy lint in the air. So there is the terror of the cannibal

machines that can also go the other way and defuse the
terror by making it pure shine and hence they are very
unpredictabl-

-e to the extent that from one moment to the next the
cannibal machine will gobble first this then that side of
the border and cast its shine here and there, hence the
terror of such machines. I mention this only because it had
become clear to me that we, I mean I and the erstwhile
bleeding women become statue ladies, had become as
one, some kind of cannibal machine, and each of us was
only one element in a larger mechanical totality that
was careering beyond any of our controls across the city
that was evidently in no state to resist our advances and,
indeed, seemed to be falling like dead heads from the
portal of a guillotine, to vary the metaphor. And though
we were as a great cannibal machine gobbling without
head, I was somehow at the same time as they say the
head, for where I moved, though I moved beyond my will,
the women would move with me, and wherever we went
we moved through walls and streets and hills and other
natural phenomena as if they were not there, although the
aforementioned phenomena themselves would be quite
affected by our passing often to the point of complete
obliteration.

Wherever we went through the city there was screaming
and terror. Though innumerable kissers and pokers and
mouthers and all the others were arrayed against us, we
swept through them as if they were not there, though, as
I said before, they were there or at least had been there
to themselves before we swept through them. Certainly,
there was something strange about finding myself in this
position since I had neither love nor power nor knowledge,

having lost all in the course of my previous encounters. I
had become something voided and weak, yet it was as if I
was at the head of a great army and a great leader, though
I did not know what I was doing, and in any case there was
no army at all just women encrusted in paint. I thought
of my dead friend the magistrate, who always knew what
he was doing, except maybe when they burnt him alive.
I did not know what the women wanted. They seemed
to have something like the essence of destruction about
them, although not destruction itself, not destruction for
destruction's sake, but because they recognised no earthly
barriers to their desire. If they knew not their desire, they
also knew not objections to it. This was

very strange, for I at least am often concerned to look
for patterns and reasons, and here indeed there were
patterns, patterns of extraordinary intricacy, but without
any discernible reason. The lack of reason of course gives
rise to any number of explanations and theories, indeed,
of expectations, for, lacking knowledge, everyone has his
or her opinion instead, convincing him or herself most
firmly to the extent that there are no real reasons for
doing so. But in and for this machine, there was no point
to opinion, for there was only action, a passive action,
in pure multiply-articulated gesture without end. There
was nothing that we did not sweep over, and wherever
we swept there was not. It seemed there could be no
resistance to us, or to whatever force it was we incarnated
or enacted. All fell before us as if there was nothing to
fall. Then, at some point, late in the afternoon, in the hazy
and exhausted air of the city, a strange sound emerged
overhead. As one, the women and I glanced up only to see
falling from the sky what seemed to be gigantic mouths
and nothing more, like organic zeppelins, like adulterated

human organs. As they fell they fell towards us with smiles breaking open the mouths that they were.

These creatures were impervious to the careering cannibal machine that I and the women had become. They began to pick us off one by one with their great mouths which bristled with all sorts of crazy teeth and fur. As they picked off the women with their great mouths, each woman would utter the most bloodcurdling and terrible of screams, and then humours of all kinds would squirt from the great mouth onto the ground where the fallen humours would burn and blacken the patch of ground upon which they fell. Then the great mouths would chomp and chew the picked-off women. Their bones could be heard crunching and grinding as the great mouths ground them up. As the women grew fewer and fewer in number the patterns that we, I and they, made as a cannibal machine, came to resemble the jerky and unnatural movements of cannibal machines grown old. This, as I have already mentioned, is inevitable even for the greatest of machines, and that is when they need to be chopped up and recomposed in other organizations with other elements. Sometimes cannibal machines die because they have grown old and tired. Sometimes they are deliberately destroyed before their power becomes too great and too destructive. Sometimes their elements need to be separated and hung up to dry pour encourager les autres as they say, like tar-soaked manikins upon gibbets or crucified slaves along the Appian

Way. Sometimes cannibal machines are destroyed in the course of other destructions. Despite their undoubted potential for power, and their name which can, of its own accord, inspire a sinister feeling or feeling of the sinister,

or indeed a sense of terror, really cannibal machines want
only, if you will permit this anthropomorphization of want,
to shine and cast the shine they cast upon the shadows
of the world without dispelling those shadows altogether.
For without shadows a cannibal machine has no reason
for being, and as pure shine forced everywhere a cannibal
machine is, as I have said, pure destruction and terror.
What I suppose I am really trying to say is something
about the very weakness of cannibal machines. Above all
their power is a tiny, flickering, near helpless power, that
relies not on kissers or pokers or magistrates or devil arse
or ambassadors or on buildings with corpses lining the
foundations or on factories or on courts, but on the almost
nothing that is pure shine, fleeting apparition amidst
shadows. To this extent a cannibal machine is constructed
to

shine as if that shine were much like love, which indeed
it is, insofar as it is pure exhaustion to pure plenitude.
But this is not a personal love, that is, a love that engages
the two and only the two, but rather a love of many for
many in the glamour of the shine, like an orgy but without
physical contact. But I have not the heart to continue this
discussion, as I was telling you about the destruction of the
cannibal machine by those immense mouths that gobbled
and drooled and spat. They had been sent to destroy
us before the whirling statuary that I and the women
comprised swallowed the whole city in our obliterating
orbit. In the end, no one gets their money back, and no
one gets to keep their soul, although they want to more
than anything. You can try all sorts of inventive rubbish in
the interim, but in the end you will disappear or be poked
or shovelled under or placed in a furnace or mouthed to
death or whatever, and this is intolerable, although a little

thought would show the same about its seeming opposite as well. Immortality is just as intolerable, for then there would be no escape into death, and without the possibility of that escape there would be only decay without end, a mug of undrinkable lukewarm

tea. Which is perhaps the case, although it may not feel like that as you are mouthed horribly to death by great mouths, as indeed the women were being mouthed now. I could not understand why those mouths were not trying to pick me myself off given that I was as available to them as any of the women. Now there were barely several of us left, and each of us was tiring, and growing weaker by the moment, and could hardly move enough to create any sort of pattern at all. Then I heard one crunch two three, and all the women were gone, gobbled up to their bones. I was alone in a landscape that, between us, I mean I and the women and the gobbling mouths, had reduced to near nothingness in our reign.

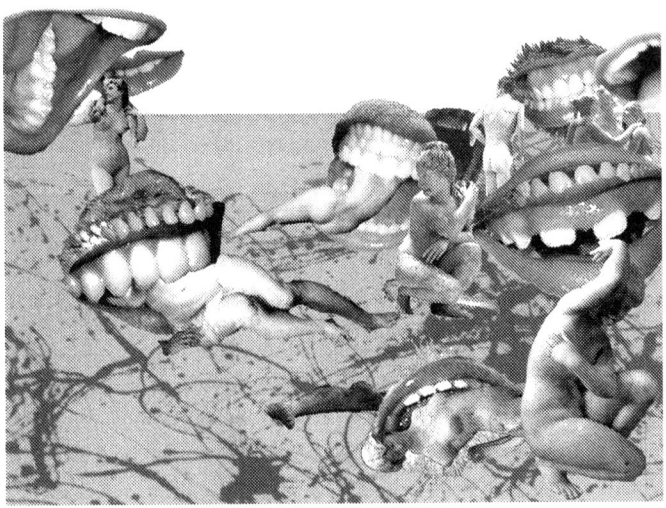

Instead of mouthing me as they had mouthed the women, the great mouths simply encircled me, and though I pushed and pushed against their great organic bulks, I was incapable of breaking out of the ring of flesh. I had become for some reason very tired, and indeed was barely able to stand at all. I was so tired that I had first to lean against the closest of the mouths. Then I squatted on the blasted ground. Finally I lay down on the earth, panting like a sick animal, the sky overhead darkening above the raw bulk of the mouths. Eventually two or three stars came out, and then more and more, spreading motionless in patterns, as if the night was an invisible face besmirched with an incurable cosmic disease, and I lay still panting on the ground, bleached entirely of strength. I had become bare life and nothing more, nothing but a body without why. I lay

there until daybreak. As the rosy tentacles of dawn twitched and wriggled across the early blue of the sky, the ring of mouths suddenly pouted, or, I should say, parted, and a slight lone figure strutted through the gap and stood over me smirking. Well, hello there, said the figure, which bore the symbols and insignia of an important government official, how are the mighty etcetera and so on, but let us leap at once and with alacrity over the pleasantries and go directly to the main point, which is, as you will no doubt already have surmised, your arrest in accordance with the laws of the city. You will be taken from here to a place of incarceration, and there kept in dolour and in sadness without hope or pity until the law sees fit to have you arraigned for trial. Then you will take your chances in the dock before the people of the city which you have so maliciously, viciously, and underhandedly attacked, and in your craven way attempted to destroy. So I reassure you,

he said coughing and blinking, I reassure you, speaking
personally now and as ahem a representative of the people
of the city, that you will be an example that is made, ahem,
an example of, for, as a great man our ambassador has said,
too many laws, not enough examples. He has, ahem, urged
us, ahem, to rectify the situation in accordance with this
dictum of enlightenment. Then he gestured brusquely at
the great mouths that had apparently slipped into a state
of quiescence so minimal they were as strange disturbing
boulders slumbering quietly on the brow of a hill. At his
sign, they roused themselves as if a strong man after sleep,

to herd me towards wherever it was they were herding
me towards. Oh, and the man said, in what he evidently
conceived to be his parting shot, I believe you remember
my very good friend and colleague the ambassador. He
has directed me to tell you that he has an interest, ahem,
yes a real interest in your case. Do not believe that he has
forgotten you, for he has not. Then the man smiled and
strutted off elsewhere, presumably on other business of
the city that he was so proud to have been delegated as a
special delegate thereof. As for myself, I was clearly in for
a different business, having now lived on the street, then
worked as a builder, then in a factory, and most recently
as an element in a cannibal machine. For some reason, the
short

trip that I enjoyed to the fetid cell promised by the
strutting official was a trip down memory lane, down
the nine lines of cot poem playing repetition present
notness others accidents love. I wondered if any of my
recent experiences had in fact been experiences, for had
I not precisely been not quite there for any of them? In
every case, I had been confused by the extremity and

unfamiliarity of the circumstances, as well as by other extenuating factors, such as not knowing, or having an opinion, or being seized as if by a greater and not necessarily conscious or intentional force. I cannot, moreover, consider such experiences or occurrences as successful passages through danger. I cannot even say if I was the same before as afterwards, nor if the dangers were real, or if leaping from the proverbial frying man into the equally proverbial was rather an intensification of the same danger, and so on. Nonetheless, I suspected that, although I was not yet there, in keeping with the promise of the ambassador through his delegate, it would be unwise to bring up such ruminations in court. That would probably be, as medical types say, counter indicated. Yet it was quite clear that I was not mad nor an idiot, nor a child, nor a mere animal, nor a kisser, nor a poker, nor possessed, although what the real differences are are anybody's guess if you'd ask me now.

This thought is probably also counter indicated. Then again, anybody ruminating on life, if anybody did, might well make the same remark about life tout court. Or then again they might not. The lassitude and despair of the previous evening having not altogether lifted, I continued to ponder my fate in such terms, until the giant pulsing mouths herded me to a gateway high and barred and wreathed around with all sorts of prohibitions and declarations proclaiming abandon all etcetera in curlicues of razor wire. T-

-here they left me to the shepherding of the guards, who were indeed shepherds of men and women if anybody could be said to be such. It was such shepherds who herded me to my promised cell that permitted a little

patch of sky to shine through as per regulation. Every now
and again the broken porcelain in the corner would also
cough as per regulation, and deposit a little trail of murky
water, often ornamented with less liquid accoutrements,
upon the concrete floor. I was particularly taken with this
porcelain amenity that in some way seemed to have taken
on a life of its own, or at least some kind of animated
vigour in the way that it ingested and expelled all sorts
of material at regular but arrhythmic intervals. What
it gave was never what it took, but had evidently been
transformed, transmuted, even transubstantiated. In time,
though, I was, I must say, still very tired, nay exhausted,
and when I say in time I have no idea how long that was,
or even how I felt about how long that was, but kept up my
system of communication with the cracked porcelain bowl
to the point where, I might even say, with justifiable pride,
that I had become a sort of scientist of its movements,
such as they

were, which were not very much, but were all the more
significant for that. For, as I say, it ingested and expelled
in a rhythm that seemed at once less-than-arbitrary and
yet without a steady beat. As I surmised, these unsteady
corporate flows must be linked to the tubes and levers and
vats of all the other amenities provided in the building,
and, as such, the rhythm of its stops and starts was clearly
linked to the rhythms of a great organization of living
creatures who were also guests and hosts of the same
institution. Even the colours of the expelled materials must
have denoted in their restricted palate or is that palette
all sorts of other factors, such as the varieties of available
foodstuff, and the emotional wellbeing of the guests and
hosts, or the malignant polyps growing inexorably in this
or that colon, or so on. Perhaps an interpretative genius

who dedicated his or her life to the study of such a field
would ultimately be able to determine from the swirl and
drip of what we might call the enigmatic tea-leaves on
the floor the proper complexity and articulation of such
events. In this pit, this cell, which spins and glows with a
light that cannot be entirely unnatural, illumined as it is by
fulgurating waters crashing helplessly against and through
the amenity that unites and divides the world, there is also
something else, something which does not shine or speak
or show itself, but

pervades everything like the clear pus that occasionally
bursts forth from a festering wound and ripples without
glistening over the skin. It was to the study of this
something else that I was now prepared to dedicate my life,
for, as they say, youth is action age reflection. Although I
was working at some disadvantage, having not the access
that I required to tools and materials, to experimental
devices and archival references, I nonetheless believe that
I got some way toward understanding the mysterious
ebb and flow of this life of the cells. In my dedication to
my chosen task, I must say that the world melted away
as it were, and I became obsessed with observation and
notation and theorisation. There is nothing in the world
that compares to such devotion or attentiveness, where
you are nothing but the observation of the little things, the
almost-nothings, the near-imperceptible differences, and
in this observation you feel yourself an integral part of the
taking-place of the whole world. It was also a condition of
complete simplicity, costing not less than everything, and,
indeed, though I was effectively absent from myself during
the period I spent in that cell observing and scratching
my observations on every available space with a little
rock to the point when the phenomena themselves began

to interfere with my scratchings. For a time there, the scratchings that I scratched were even submerged beneath the shallow, almost infinitesimal, waves of phenomena that issued from the amenity, so I cannot, therefore, always vouch for their veracity. Despite resting for a long time in that cell, I was still surprisingly

tired, nay, exhausted. For though I suppose that I did not move very much in my cell, the effort of observing so minutely is always an expenditure of more energy than it may seem to casual onlookers, of which, in this case, there were probably none. Although my shepherds did stick their crooks in the door every now and then, an action which I presume was, as were most things, per regulation, and occasionally throw me scraps of foodstuff, for the most part I was left entirely to my own devices. These for the most part, as I have been saying, involved observing. The situation was entirely to the benefit of science as it happens, for many breakthroughs that I made would have been otherwise impossible if I had not been free to dedicate myself without distractions to the tasks at hand. Any diminution or lapse in concentration would certainly have set back my painstaking observations to an infelicitous degree. Indeed,

when the shepherds of men and women came to the door of my promised cell and with rough entreaties enticed me to the door, I was at first appalled and rebellious, and resisted with all my strength, as my observations had reached such a critical point that I was certain that, with only one or two further observations, the solution to the enigma of the arrhythmic amenity would be firmly within my grasp. But it was not to be, and, though I clung to the stained porcelain, praying desperately that perhaps there would one day be research institutions of the future dedicated to retrieving restoring preserving and displaying such important scratchings as were mine, much as archaeologists have hitherto expended so much energy on those fragmentary papyri and incomprehensible remnants of antiquity, I was nonetheless briskly removed from the cell in which I had spent so many productive days weeks months whatever

and bustled into a waiting transportation which was without windows for me to look out. The engine started, and I was borne for hours over uneven ground, being shaken about inside as if in a ride at a fairground, but without me caring to enjoy it. During that time there was nothing to do except be bumped about. At several points I, or rather my head, even bounced lazily off the roof as it, my head that is, were a ball, but a ball that could not help thinking that it was nothing but a ball, now that everything was really gone, my parents loved sign magistrate women study of the amenity and all that was left to me were my memories cot poem playing repetition present notness others accidents love but they seemed to be stripped of any tie even to what had gone that I was nothing but a ball stripped of all but itself. But as a ball I was not stripped of feeling. On the contrary, I felt enormous pain, as if an anaesthetic that I did not realise that I had had had finally worn off, although the wound, whatever it was, was still fresh. I suffered the wound of myself as a ball with nothing for the remainder of that ride without

relief. I felt as if there had been a forcible intrusion like a knife cutting into its victim, but there was neither knife nor memory of a knife, only the pain of its intrusion. Even when the vehicle had stopped, and I was bustled out again with the same efficiency with which I had been placed in it in the first place, and thence through an open door that resembled the little opening of a servant's entrance at the back of a grand household, and thence down a fetid and dimly lit corridor, the black and white tiling of which had been permitted to wear and crack with ostentatious disuse, and thence up a little staircase to a much grander corridor with carpet and dark wood groining, and thence through a pair of heavy doors into what could only be described as chambers, whereupon I was abandoned by the shepherds to the ministrations of the figures already waiting for me there, I still felt that pain. There were three figures in those chambers. One was grotesquely overweight, like an engorged buffoon whose consumption had driven him to performing at children's parties. The buffoon had two slimmer accompanists, one male, one female, both with little white curls that curled gently about their ears. They shared physiognomical features that one could only describe

as comfortable and comforting. Well hallo, here's the famous indigent troublemaker, hoffed the fat one happily, you don't at all resemble the pictures we have built up from the stories. Perhaps they have been treating you roughly in confinement, I shouldn't be surprised, or maybe the stories have just enlarged your person to a paper leviathan you never were, well I can assure you whatever is the case you'll have your fair day in court hof hof. Then, for the benefit of his two friends, he slung a jocular arm about me to show that he was a friend of the people, and while he understood my actions, whatever he perceived them to be, he would not let an indefinable sense of affinity sway his better judgement nor his august judicial responsibilities nor of course his profound love of justice. Well, here you have your adversary, rumbled the man, gesturing at the becurled man with one swollen red paw, he is not your friend at all, are you my good man. At that point I heard a faint noise in the background which sounded like many persons murmuring with anticipation, but could not tell how close or far it was from where we were. The becurled man offered me a slim smile to show no hard feelings, that's just the way things go, and in other circumstances perhaps it would all have been different, etcetera. Having proffered this genuine token of warmth he stepped back gently for the other to approach.

Now this is your friend, remarked the florid arbiter, gesturing brusquely with his hand towards the woman with curls who had just stepped forward to bleat happily at me, and this, don't forget, he reminded me, is your adversary, and he gestured likewise towards the man with curls who bleated just as happily, and, just as he had before, without malice or forethought. Then, the introductions and friendly reminders done, they all bleated happily at one another as they had no doubt done

for many years. After they had bleated happily for some time, the fat buffoon smiled genially and said much as I would like to continue this warm discussion indefinitely, we have unfortunately a great deal of business to which to attend, and he called to the shepherds, who, though I had not noticed, had been waiting patiently outside the great double doors, that those shepherds should escort myself and my new friend into court. They, that is, the shepherds, at once obeyed, and herded us through a small side door into the aforementioned court, and at once I was struck dumb by its size and noise and the vast numbers of persons who were there, some obviously with official functions, such as the sucking lady, but more just there as if a vast and entertaining spectacle was to be staged for their edification and enjoyment. My friend began to bleat as if spontaneously, for she was so in her element that it was as green fields and blue skies to a pastoral poet, and she veritably gambolled to her seat, which was worn and still warm from the many years in which she had occupied it with her excitement and her happiness. I, however, was directed to stand in a tiny central construction, a little wooden stand with bars.

All eyes were upon me in wonder and fear, and I could feel the weight of my fate already pressing down upon me, carried by the wonder of those eyes. Then all were told to rise, and we rose, and the fat arbiter waddled in and sat, and we all sat except for myself, for I was forced to stand in the dock because, I presume, that is natural for the accused who ought never rest beneath the scrutiny of the law. Then the trial, such as it was, began with the reading of all sorts of charges and indictments against me. In response, there were all sorts of disquisitions upon and objections against the niceties of treating my personage in just this way, for the most part delivered in the strange but somehow legible bleating voices of those with curls. The voices bleated on and on, endless, and, at least, I thought in the course of that trial, I could trust that injustice would be done. After all, the soul is only the ghost of its nomination. Many of the assembled began snuffling about in their neighbour's bodies in response to the excitement engendered by the prosecution's bleating, but I had unfortunately become very bored by the endlessness of the proceedings that were

making me miss my work in my cell. Then, of course, I remembered my journey here. I pondered whether the real horror is, like the cell, elsewhere and unanimous. At least my physical pain had subsided. As for the boredom, I realised, somewhere in the midst of the bleating, that it was a spasm, a spasm that defends. Boredom is a difficult technique forged in the furnace, if you'll pardon the mixed metaphor, of the long march of civilisation. The bread and wine of civilisation is boredom, and the saviour of such a civilisation would never die but rather could never be bothered to do so. Every now and again a bleated phrase would intrude into my apathy, a phrase of the order of *satisfactory castigation is impracticable for such bad actions* or *rivers of blood and vast tribulation* or some such, but I could not even care to shrug in the spasms of boredom that had possessed me. Something strange slowly washed over and enveloped me like the black ink of an octopus, as I stood there in the stand, and I felt above all like screaming out the story of my experiences, such as they were. I felt that then I would have at least told the truth before the court and its very many customers, even if I myself proved the false element of my tale. So I began as I began with you.

The first thing I remember is that I had climbed from my cot over the bars and under the whirling turbulence of the mobiles that hung above like paper constellations of animals of which I knew nothing. I was a child, an infant, a baby, and those mobiles were not images. I knew not lions and snakes and monkeys and goats, those creatures that the others saw. I knew only anythings, frightful coloured smears that whirred and spun, the spongy mat of my bed, the rasping wood of the bars. So out I climbed. I ran around and around in the room, overjoyed to be beyond the bars and the endless swing and rock of the false animals suspended from the ceiling that was high as any ceiling might be.

And I remember the sounds, the feet and voices outside, outside the room of my cot and my freedom, and I knew then that I should be behind the bars for the good of us all. I ran and ran to the cot and climbed and climbed like I was climbing the sheer abyss of hell before its fall so I could feign the incarceration that pleases all but my feet were slippery on the rungs of the cot. And I remember the panic as I scrabbled and scrabbled with my scrabbling feet on the rungs of the cot, as behind me the sound of the heavy feet and the voices grew and I panicked as I felt the air of the opened door behind me and the breath of those people heavy heavy on my little neck as I fell screaming to the cot that had not held me. If only it had held me. They had seen me and they too were screaming that I had not been held and were mad. And

so I went on and on, and when I had finished my tale, which was exactly as I have told it to you, everyone was in disarray. They did not know what to do or how to proceed, because, as it seemed, nothing like this was acceptable according to the rules of the court. All of a sudden, a door flew open, and the ambassador who I had not seen since childhood strode in. Immediately the pain in my ear flared from the spittle he had deposited there so many years ago. I screamed not only with the pain, but with a rage that I did not know that I possessed. With the unexpected apparition of the ambassador, everyone fell silent. Although it was clear he should have no jurisdiction here, in reality, he was as everyone knew the favoured representative of the government in its entirety, and, as it turns out, a representative more powerful than the organ he represented. In the years in which I had not seen him, he had grown in stature. He had grown more arms and legs, none of them human, to the point where he was now a gargantuan ball of grotesque and inexplicable functions. When he saw me seeing him as if anew, he smiled with many of his many mouths. From within one of those mouths protruded another mouth on a stalk, and, with an icy flash of terror, I recognised that mouth as the very mouth that had whispered in my ear all those years ago. Even though I was incarcerated in this dock and could not move, I would have been unable to move anyway, paralysed as I was by that oh unforgotten apparition. O my friend, it whispered lasciviously, did I not say that we would meet again, and that you and I would work together as if seamlessly, though it look unlike. I think, it continued, that we have worked together long enough, and that there is nothing much more that you can do for me, though we have had a time, haven't we. And a-

-ll gazed on him with admiration, though I am uncertain whether they had heard what he had said to me from his mouth on a stalk that had come from another mouth. After they had had their fill of gazing, which seemed to last an indecent length of time, they began all at once to chatter excitedly, and the sucking woman began to type with a crazy intensity, and the white curls began to bleat bleat bleat. The ambassador ignored their chattering and bleating and importunings, for he had other things he wished to say to me. Most important, he said, is that you realise that though you think the black river is the antithesis of the spittle that I deposited in your ear, they are in fact cousins, and more than cousins, more like kissing cousins. Depending on the places inside where the black river runs, the organism will do different things. You, I know, are close to the black river, and to the creatures that come from the other side. So you must be swayed, for the black river is nothing for this world, though all feel its excitement and its power. Yet it is too raw for kissers and pokers and what-have-you, for they would not be as they are if they dipped their toes in the black rive-

-r. Then, to the approbation of all in the court, he extended his tendrils and stripped my clothes from me because, he said, with a mouth that spoke things that do not happen in order that all could hear, I would not be needing them where I was going. They would be better used by people who would use them not for theft and murder and every bad thing that all had adjudged that I was pre-eminently guilty of, but to abide with the law. He opened another mouth that had until then been hidden, and swallowed the clothes that I had been wearing, many of which I had carried with me since the disappearance of my parents. All in a trice my clothes were gone just like that. I was naked before the court, and all in the room cackled and shouted that I should throw myself on the mercy of the court, because the ambassador had shown everybody the guilt that I had been concealing within me. That guilt was now exposed to the clean air of the court, and justice would be done because the cat, as the phrase has it, was now out of the bag and it was a guilty cat if they had ever seen one. I saw myself as I was in their eyes, and I saw the disgust and shame of myself, and could not help but burst into tears though I tried as hard as I could to blink them back. There

was no question that, once my guilt had been so exposed, then the shame beneath the guilt was also brought to light, and mingled, moreover, with the shame was something like anxiety and a feeling of disgust so dark it seemed even like the black river which had guided my life had been nothing but that deeply concealed sense of disgust and so as nothing really, nothing. So even the creatures from the other side that had engulfed innumerable souls were mere figment, and not from a realm more true than that of this court. Those assembled in the court saw my guilt and my shame and my anxiety and my self-disgust, and all howled that these were nothing more than the derisory twitchings of a meagre individual soul who knew nothing whatsoever of the world, and had simply gone astray like a wee idiot lamb. One among them yelled out that this meant also that there were no kissers and no pokers and no bleaters and no sucking woman and no man with a metal claw for a tongue. The world was really just full of individuals each with their own little pleasures and pains, and yet they were real individuals, part of the wonderful if sometimes stormy and troubled story of humankind. All bellowed their assent, and even the ambassador shook his many tentacles as if in fervent agreement with the declaration. As if

the scales had fallen from my eyes I fell naked to my knees and begged forgiveness from the howling court. They all cried as one, not yet, not yet, you have further to go, further yet, and so I looked more carefully and more closely at the innards of me that had been so exposed. I began to analyse the striations and sedimentations within the guilt and the shame and the anxiety and the self-disgust, and as I looked more and more microscopic layers revealed themselves to my gaze. Each layer was as complex as an entire world, no, more, a universe, and each universe was composed of infinite universes in its turn. I broke down and confessed that it was not in my power, nor was there time enough in any universe to tell all the horror of any level of mine. Each pond and each garden contains other ponds and gardens with their own fish and flowers and each fish and flower is itself such a garden and such a pond. To which the court responded as one with a smile of satisfaction, as if I had finally learned the most valuable of lessons. If only I had, as others had, known it from early on, then none of this would have happened, and I would not be here but still living with my pare-

-nts. I would never have thought that people were wrong signs, for they are not. I would never have thought that there were nine memories cot poem playing repetition present notness others accidents love, for there are not. As I wept, I felt for a moment a simple oneness with the assembled, and even with the ambassador. Now he seemed not a monster at all, but a mere person who had given his life over to public affairs and to the public good at no small sacrifice to himself. Indeed, he had made a sacrifice of the best sort, one which thought sacrifice only worthwhile if it was possible to help others just as he had helped me now, his sacrifice validated by my present salvation just now in the court. Everyone was happy and balloons were released and music played. The public was momentarily at one. But before it was possible for me to enjoy in any real way this new feeling of oneness with the people, the black river rose inside me again. I felt its ice and its heat and its pure indifference greater than anything, and knew that it would in the final instance corrode me the court even the ambassador as tremulous fragile bodies in an acid bath without a second thought. The black river was

not a lie, and neither were the creatures from the other side, with their humming voices and stench of rot and carrion and corpses, and it was not altogether I or I alone who had suffered this guilt and this shame and this anxiety and self-disgust. No, these are the hallmarks of mortals who must never cross the river until the holes that they are dissolve in its nothingness. I realised that the revelation of my guilt and shame and self-disgust was nothing of the kind. It had merely been the last resort of a court desperate to make me believe in it. These things had nothing to do with me. They are only wrong signs of wrong signs that everyone is to be made to share and then pretend they do not. When I knew that I knew this, this ambassador's spittle in my ear burst again into flame. The feeling of it had almost disappeared when I had thought that the shame was mine. This was another sign that the black river was real. Otherwise, the spittle could have had no efficacy if it had not shared a complicity with a force greater than itself. The revelation of my guilt was a sham. Only the black river was real, but not any the less horrible or terrifying for that,

and so were the creatures of the other side. I realised that if I did not keep quiet as the phrase has it about the truth of the river and the others, then all the good feeling would dissipate or vaporize like so much nothingness in the air, and every member of the court would turn against me, and even my bleating friend would bleat and bleat in my face until I passed out from the bleating and did I really want to do that to them after making them all so happy with my confession. Indeed, the little taste of oneness, one might even say pure communion, I had just experienced after my public acknowledgement of my guilt and shame and anxiety and self-disgust was something that I was loathe to give up. I had never previously felt such happiness, and it was indeed nice. So I vacillated in myself, and as I did the pain in my ear grew steadily, no, exponentially, in intensity, and I noticed that the ambassador had noticed my vacillation, and a frown came over his many mouths, and his tentacles writhed in displea-

-ure. Though I could barely think from the pain of the ambassador's spittle in my ear, and though I knew that it would die away again in an instant if only I embraced my self-disgust again, I could not. For I thought of my memories cot poem playing repetition present notness others accidents love, that, if no use to anyone, least of all myself, would be betrayed if I embraced my self-disgust. So I forced myself to stutter out an impromptu recantation of my recent recantation to the court. Whereupon everything fell at once silent, and every balloon simultaneously burst, raining down sticky fragments of deliquescent rubber upon the assembled personages. The ambassador glowered and swelled with an anger that I would have thought unimaginable, and too great for any human being to contain, until I remembered that he was of course not really a human being at all, and that though he seemed on the verge of doing so he was not about to burst like the aforementioned balloons. Oh

the furore that erupted after that instant of weakness on my part was greater than the baying of the magistrate or of devil arse or the bleeding women bringing down the factory of our incarceration or the ring of mouths, and I have never heard such commotion, such lamentation and wailing. Not that it was lamentation and wailing really, for really I sensed a deep satisfaction. Now I knew they knew they would have my blood, and on the unimpeachable grounds so to speak of my recantation of my recantation. There are images I have seen of two brothers of wit who were flayed alive and disembowelled by an angry mob because they prayed for calm and freedom, and even in the sadness and horror of those little images presented by sympathisers of the murdered one can still reel with mingled emotions from the residues of the ecstasy the mob must have experienced in tearing them apart. That was the sense that I now had. I would be torn apart like those two brothers,

whose dream was freedom, whose fate was martyrdom for

nothing. Yet this was after all a court of law, so when the ambassador declared to the unbridled admiration of the court that terror is the piety of the people, it was rather as a preamble to another altogether more solemn and traditional address. This address is that of the sentence of death. For the sentence of death is the very foundation of law, and is hallowed. In order for such sentence to be properly executed, it is necessary that its speaker assume an orotund and saddened tone which gives the impression that it is important to give the impression of the sanctity of life and of the melancholy of its extinction, although extinction of a life is precisely what the sentence is aiming at. The court for the most part calmed down at this sentence of death. The ambassador had produced several black hoods which he must have had secreted about his person for just such an eventuality, and he placed these on various of his heads during the sentencing itself. The calm was undoubtedly due to this traditional solemnity that chastened all present, and made them reflect ruefully upon the transience of life, and the ashes to ashes nature of existence. Which

of course is not to say that they were not profoundly gladdened by the promise and anticipation of my death, and in fact I know, despite the shocked silence, they would have been disappointed if I had ultimately wriggled out of having to die by truly submitting myself to the mercy of the court, as I had momentarily done just before. I must admit to a slight puzzlement at the sentence, however. Because, as you have seen, there was no question that I was guilty of many things, it was still not clear for what exactly I was being tried. Of the interminable list of charges against me that had been read before, none were really what you would call a hanging offence. But the puzzlement quickly passed, as there were many other issues to concentrate the mind. In fact, the very superfluity of particular laws in the face of the demands of the law itself needs no weighty ponderings to be obvious to all. Not to mention the many benefits of a weighty judgement directed against a loathsome malfeasant, which is always a crowd-pleaser. Perhaps it is the very gap between the guilt and the preposterousness of the sentence that pleases so. After all, everybody is undoubtedly guilty of many things, so a disproportionate sentence ensures you get what's coming to you, if under another unrecognisable name. Who can be sure that guilt punished in its own name would smell as sweet. Oh

there were many furrowed brows and much head-shaking following the sentence being handed down. A court is nothing other than an engine or organism of the truth, as well as its dramatic theatre. So the professed sadness of the passing of a life is balanced by a satisfaction at the fact that, despite the terrible state of the world, injustice can still be done. Counting up all I had accomplished in my stay in that court room, you could say that I had provided my audience with a unspecifiable sense of excitement and spectacle, colour and movement, and a good feeling about their own philanthropy in saving me, and another sort of good feeling about how shocked they were when I refused to be saved, and another feeling of righteous good fury at my mocking of the court, and yet another good feeling, that of raw blood lust, and, before I forget, a feeling of pensive existential languor

and also a sense of injustice satisfied. The whole time the spit in my ear was burning, yet I felt strangely dissociated from the whole thing, even when several of the ladies in the audience burst into tears when the ambassador, still wearing his several black hoods, speculated on the details of my ill-deeds, and spoke of how they would strap me into a chair and run electricity through my body while I shook and ejected my innards like a little child and fried and fried like a bad egg. At that, the sucking lady erupted in a frenzy of sucking, and all the white curls bleated like a colloquy of the herds, and kissers of all kinds streamed through the court kissing like there was no tomorrow, slobbering saliva on the most diverse body parts. The ambassador squatted over all, and was pleased as anything that

he did not have long to wait before the consummation of his promise to me when I was a child. Then he himself escorted me from the court along a corridor that grew narrower and narrower as we went until it terminated in a cell that was nothing but bars and seemed to hang in the air without support. He said to me that this was to be my last night on earth, and reminded me that I had done good by him, so good that I had helped him to acquire kissers and pokers and possessed, and helped to destroy rival magistrates and my own love and lead an army of rebellion that he could easily defeat to his own glory. Finally, he was very happy that he could try me himself, though I had been a mere tool in his tentacles, and that no one would ever know, as everything appeared different from the way it really was. As he said this I trembled with helplessness, and cursed again the black river and the creatures from the other side who had helped him curb and mould me though I struggled to escape. Every escape had been delusion, just another nail in the stumbling coffin of myself. The ambassador laughed at my cursing, and said that I had now truly recanted my recantation of my recantation. Now I truly knew that I had been right to recant the first time, if only to save myself. But now it was too lat-

-e, and my indecision was my downfall. I had not even fallen with pride and integrity, but as something that snivelled and was a butt of shame. That was the moment at which I felt worst of all. I felt as bad as when I found my parents gone or when I betrayed my love or when they burnt the magistrate alive or when the women were mouthed to death around me or when I experienced the pain of a non-existent knife or when my shame and self-disgust were exposed to the mercy of the court. For it was true I had been the instrument of my own destruction, just as I had seen so many others skin themselves alive each in their own way. Whereupon, I fell as if fainting. In my brief faint I caught a whiff of the rot that the creatures of the other side bear within them. I awoke at once, and, as my eyes flickered open, I caught the ambassador's eyes and he too somehow caught a whiff of the stench of the engulfed rotting innards that repeat in the bellies of the creatures of the other side, and I saw him flinch, though he was many-mouthed and great. Then I knew that I could recant again or not with equal legitimacy, and that, despite my fate being sealed as if the signet had already impressed itself upon the soft red wax, the ambassador had been lucky. Despite everything, the little memories that were mine were enough to unseat him. A vision came to me. In the end, he would end up dissolving in the acid of the river more fearful than I just a moment be-

-fore. At once I smiled at him. He leapt back, outraged and confused, and I kept smiling though the spittle he had lodged in my ear since childhood had never burned with such a flame, and he stumbled backwards along the corridor with his many mouths each crying for the executioners to come. Out they sprang with their enormous eyes and hands like prongs and pincers and things that tear and shatter. They seized and bound me and dragged me along that final corridor to the place of the chair. They handled me so roughly that their glittering sharp hands sank into my flesh at so many points that when I got to the chair I was raw and bleeding from every pore, and though I was less in substance I was more in pain. Despite the pain I was almost in a delirium like that of the mystics, and because of all the blood the executioners' hands kept slipping as they tried to strap me into the chair. This meant that they tore more and more from my body, which was disappearing at an alarming rate, and at that rate there would soon be nothing left of me to electrocute. They became more and more desperate, convinced that they had botched the execution. I was now barely a skeleton wreathed in a water-thin winding-sheet of blood. Though it would still be an execution, something had gone awry, and even the executioners could sense that the ambassador himself was spooked by the stripping-bare of my flesh. This, after all, did not speak well of the supposed majestic indifference of the sentence of the court, but insinuated all manner of pettier concerns. Yet, as they say, the die was cast, and there was no going back now. Somehow finally they got me into the chair. As they strapped me in

I thought of another possibility. This was that the black river and the burning spittle in my ear which still hurt more than the rest of me though I had been to all intents and purposes skinned alive were more than simply cousins and that the black river was nothing natural nor supernatural, but was just the shall-we-say inheritance of humanness, in that the burning spittle was to be added to

that river by my death, and that the river was composed
of the spittle of other ambassadors that every previous
generation had had deposited in its ears or indeed in any
of its other orifices, and though it had probably begun
as a trickle it had become the great river that now it was.
It would never cease to grow in strength and size with
every generation, until it was impossible even to pretend
to escape its claims by kissing or poking or whatever. In
the end the black river would burst its banks to become a
black sea whose centre was everywhere and circumference
nowhere. That would surely be the ultimate disaster, the
apocalypse, but, at the same time, the end of the river
itself, for all humanity would have been dissolved, and the
river or the sea or the blackness needs humans, for though
they are its creatures it lives only in and through them.
But there was no time for further speculations, for the
executioners had strapped me in

and they put the screws on me and they put me in a big
white nappy like I was a little child again in my cot. But
this is not a cot with bars, and there is the hot breath of the
big people who I cannot see behind me on my neck and I
am already shaking as I hear the creatures of the other side
streaming over the black river in their thousands and in
their hundreds of thousands and oh I have never seen so
many of them before or heard their engulfed souls rustling
like the chitinous rustling of putrescent insects and the
stench of their coming is awful and they are keening they
are keening those creatures of the other side with their
rotting souls why are they keening and behind their thin
cries the spittle of the ambassador is burning again like
poison in my ear and it is as if all my body is being kissed
by great bundles of tongues and I look up and see through
the great glass a wall of white faces smirking their eyes like

black holes that buzz and flutter like absent fire flies and their eyes are in my eyes and the rot of carrion is in my nostrils and the spit is burning in my ear and the keening is in my ears and behind the keening the black river roars and there is pain in my body such pain as you could not imagine and it hurts I feel the black river shaking I feel the black river shaking and the pain is wearing the hole that I am away and the hole is washing away into the black river that shakes and runs and it is into the black river that I flow the black river flowing shaking the black river flowing now the black river shaken black

www.ingramcontent.com/pod-product-compliance
Ingram Content Group UK Ltd.
Pitfield, Milton Keynes, MK11 3LW, UK
UKHW021257180426
11947UKWH00015B/891